About the Author

Richard Jarvis served for many years as a London police officer within the Metropolitan Police Service. He also has gained considerable experience within the transport industry.

Primarily working face to face with the public, Richard's observations of people's behaviour has led him to study psychotherapy and popular psychology. He has a passion for travel and history as well as a passive interest in the paranormal. Richard lives in East Sussex.

The Cave Girl Files

Richard Jarvis

The Cave Girl Files

Olympia Publishers
London

www.olympiapublishers.com
OLYMPIA PAPERBACK EDITION

A CIP catalogue record for this title is
available from the British Library.

ISBN: 978-1-80074-091-4

First Published in 2021

Olympia Publishers
Tallis House
2 Tallis Street
London
EC4Y 0AB

Printed in Great Britain

Dedication

I dedicate this book to my wonderful children: William, Molly, Freddie and Hugo.

For Di – I will be forever grateful for your acts of patience, support and selfless bravery during the times we were hiding in the 'safe house', and for cooking my dinner whilst you kept lookout for those who were out to silence me. Without you, the truth would never have been revealed.

Love to you always.

Acknowledgements

The author would like to express his gratitude to Mr Hugh Jackson of Jackson Proofreading Services, Lewes, East Sussex for his assistance.

Additionally, the loyalty dedication to duty and exemplary conduct of Sneekaboo, Geekaboo and Raaahh will always be appreciated. Special mention is made to Peekaboo for outstanding diplomacy in the facilitation of all communications and engagements with former US President Donald Trump. (Maybe Joe Biden will be of sound mind Peeka).

CHAPTER ONE
SKYLIE AND FRIENDS

'She's just ripped his arm off!'

'Is this part of the act?'

'I'm not sure that it is. The music has stopped. People should run away, and the security blokes are getting beaten up by those girls!'

'Those women are like wild animals; how can they be so strong? She's just broken his neck and thrown him a hundred yards!'

'Yeah, he doesn't look good. He's not moving. Run!'

Thankfully, the shock, utter chaos and subsequent brilliant music masked the sheer brutality of what in fact was taking place and largely spared those present from fully comprehending the complete horror of the experience.

On Saturday 25th August 1984, an audience of nearly 60,000 had gathered within Rother Varley Country Park in South Yorkshire to watch a particularly successful and lucrative T. Rex tribute band perform at an outdoor event. The dishonest promotors had managed to swell ticket sales at inflated prices by falsely claiming that American wrestler, Hulk Hogan would be joining the band on stage, as a means of elevating his music career.

Two independent eyewitnesses (a high court judge and a church minister) separately reported that at exactly 9.30 p.m., with *Get It On* being performed, a gang of five women were standing together, a considerable distance from the stage and the bulk of the crowd. Both observers stated that the girls began to sprint across the grass fields towards the stage at a speed of around eighty m.p.h.!

For the fans having fun in the warm weather and enjoying the music of such a popular band, what was to follow must have felt like the start of Armageddon. In unison, all five female gang members frenziedly punched, thumped, kicked, scratched, bit and poked thousands of people in the crowd. Still not satisfied with people dropping like flies and the death toll mounting at an alarming rate, the level of slaughter was to be accelerated to an industrial level when a petite new woman, singing a song containing the lyrics 'I'm spinning around' joined them, at which point one of the women screamed with excitement: 'Great idea, Skylie!' Then, with military precision and timing, the women spontaneously held out their arms horizontally to each side and began spinning their bodies at such velocity, that each girl had effectively transformed into a propeller as powerful and destructive as one attached to an aircraft engine revving at full throttle!

As T. Rex's adoring fans had packed themselves as close to the stage as possible, this area was the most densely populated. However, the 'spinning around' method proved amazingly effective as the women cut through the crowd like knives through butter — or, as in this case, as propellers through flesh! As for the live band, well, any egoistic pleasure when performing to an appreciative audience evaporated in an instant. Panic and terror now prevailed. The professional musicians had smugly considered themselves 'talented' and 'cool', certainly deserving of considerable wealth and a 'champagne lifestyle', and they had enjoyed both, much to the envy of all other tribute acts. But those days were over!

As the women athletically jumped onto the platform, the band members knew these were no swooning, giggly teenagers. For a brief period, T. Rex held centre stage; however, there was little doubt as to who was going to steal the show, and with an unforgettable display of 'girl power'! The tribute members pathetically begged for their lives, oblivious to the fact that the handheld microphones they were holding in such a vice-like grip were still on and the sound levels from the venue were to increase tenfold!

The huge, commercial-specification speakers emitted the terrible, piercing noise of the men screaming as the women placed their hands upon the heads of the pop stars and squeezed. The volume was such, I subsequently discovered, that people fifty miles away suffered hearing loss. Relief from this sustained, hellish and utterly ghastly noise eventually came when the speakers themselves were unable to tolerate the sound for one single second longer and 'blew'.

The expression on the girls' faces displayed obvious amusement upon discovering that the involuntary sounds coming from the band members could be varied, depending on the degree of pressure and location on the scalp applied. Despite the loss of acoustic equipment, the women then took delight in their playing of 'human musical instruments' and created a melody consisting of more screaming, crying, groaning and howling. A woman with dark hair and an American accent, the apparent ringleader, quipped, 'Ha, that's our latest hit... "Head Massage"! We are nasty little trolls. Now we just need to give ourselves a stage name. Oh yes! I know: Skylie and the Pussycat Trolls. Good job, girls!'

Upon the release of the women's fingers, the T. Rex tributaries thudded onto the stage floor, silent and motionless. Then, after high-fiving her friends in celebration, the ringleader stamped her foot on the head of a band member. With a sickening crack from his skull, blood and brain particles poured onto the stage. This was the cue for the other women to do the same. With just the lead singer, Henry Teague, left, a blonde would-be executioner approached his prostrate body and, just as her foot hovered above Henry's head, she slipped over on spilt blood. As she returned to her feet, the dark-haired one joked, 'Oh, Cimberley, you're such a dizzy blonde.'

'I know I can be a bit dizzy, Nicola. How embarrassing was that?' replied Cimberley, also with an American accent.

Being a 'dizzy blonde', she had not just slipped over; remembering to finish Henry off had also slipped her mind. Instead, Cimberley used her foot to push Henry around, using his body as a broom to sweep up blood, brains and corpses. With the stage now clear, she continued the sweeping motion of her foot to propel Henry ten miles across the sky. Unconscious, he bounced off a trampoline in a rear garden, shot through the open window of a house in a neighbouring street and fell onto an empty bed before arriving in hospital by ambulance. Meanwhile, back at the concert, Cimberley looked down to survey the stage and said, 'Now that's a bit less mess. I hate clutter.'

People at the concert who were still alive included fans, sound technicians, lighting engineers and security staff. All were incapacitated from such a deep shock that they were unable to either escape or offer any form of resistance to those extraordinary women. In fact, the much-acclaimed T. Rex tribute band ended up being a mere warm-up act for Skylie and the Pussycat Trolls, who wasted no time in retrieving the abandoned electric guitars and, after one or two sparks and the obligatory 'Testing, testing, one, two, three', had the giant speakers back to full working order! And so, the audience were treated to a medley of absolute belters, including a very catchy little number, 'Don't Cha Cha Cha Cha'. In fact, the girls had been so good that a psychic medium I spoke to years later said, 'All the people who attended the gig and had been alive when Skylie and the Pussycat Trolls sang and danced were glad they were there.' Such high praise from beyond the grave indicates the supreme quality of the entertainment the women put on that remarkable day! The name of the medium was Derrick, and he had the most awful accent, suggesting to me he was originally from Bootle, Lancashire.

By the time the authorities were alerted, Skylie and the Pussycat Trolls were long gone. Police were able to take verbal accounts from the seriously injured judge and church minister, who both sadly died whilst singing 'Don't Cha Cha Cha Cha' to the officers. I believe we should take some small comfort, however, in that they'd both confirmed to the police, that, 'It was all worthwhile just to hear the girls sing and see such amazing dancing.' Unfortunately, the severity of their injuries had resulted in the men of the judiciary and cloth passing away, before written statements could be obtained, but it was confirmed that, in the absence of Hulk Hogan, the women decided to provide yet further entertainment by wrestling with their apparent new fans.

Henry suffered long-term, life-changing injuries at the hands of these women and was the only survivor, but I know there is a part of him that wishes he had heard them sing live. Poor Henry.

I first became aware of the South Yorkshire incident whilst living in the United States and holding the position of Professor of Public Engagement of the University of Washington. My parents back home in England informed me by telephone that my friend Henry Teague (a T. Rex tribute artist) was critically ill in hospital, having been the victim of a road traffic accident. They had no further information as, according to Henry's family, 'the police were being very cagy, and it all seemed a little fishy'.

However, I had a photo shoot arranged the next day for my entry to the 'Stupid-Looking Scientist of the Year Competition' and was due to travel to the Middle East to lead an expedition to completely unchartered territory within a week. The timing of Henry's incident was certain to also delay a meeting with the editor of *Scientific American* magazine (where I had a regular column: 'Professor Bond's Brilliant Breakthroughs'). However, I knew Henry was the priority. After all, we had known each other since primary school. He was my best friend. He was my only friend. He owed me £10.

The Henry Teague I knew was blessed with devilishly-handsome looks and charisma to match. Knowing his body was likely to be badly broken and he was seriously ill, I had prepared myself for him to be far from his best. Nonetheless, what I saw in the hospital ward shook me like a leaf. For sitting in there, were the most grotesquely, disfigured features I had ever witnessed. As I tentatively approached, I whispered, 'Oh, Henry, what has happened to you, my dear friend?' There were two eyes and possibly even a face. It seemed to be positive that he was out of bed, and 'Henry' was written on him, so maybe he had been at least able to supply them his name. But he was very shrunken in height and his arms and legs were missing. That terrible red colour? He must have lost his skin — and what is that long, black thing on him? I concluded that it must be a removable feeding or breathing tube that the surgeons had attached. 'Henry, I'm so terribly sorry for what has become of you. When you feel up to it, we can talk about that £10 you owe me. By the look of things, you will die soon.'

Upon sensing a presence, I turned around. 'Are you here for Henry?' asked an auxiliary nurse with flaming red hair. Before I could confirm, she added with what some described as her delightful County Galway mispronunciation and accent, 'By Jesse, that's tree times I've asked for that Henry Hoover to be put away!' Mistaking an overpaid musician for a vacuum cleaner... easily done, I consoled myself! I followed her as she walked towards a private room. 'Henry's in here,' she said.

'By the way, you should say "three" not "tree". "Thirty" not "terty". Try practising. You haven't just stepped off the boat from Ireland during the nineteenth century,' I rebuked.

So, for several hours, I sat next to the hospital bed in which Henry lay. I gazed at him, then gazed around the room, back at him and then out of the window. Occasionally a nurse would enter to complete her observations; she would smile at me before leaving me to do my gazing and listen to the hypnotic beeps of Henry's life support machine.

From being motionless and in apparent deep sleep,

Henry's body began to twitch, and his eyelids started to flicker. At first, he was restless but then became agitated, fighting with the sheet. 'Henry, are you awake? Are you awake? It's your friend Crawford. Crawford Bond, the professor. Can you hear me?' As he seemed to acknowledge I was with him, I continued. 'Wake up, Henry. You owe me £10; you do not want to die owing me money. I want my money back.' Henry began to sigh in irritation. Not to be palmed off, I began speaking with a firmer tone. 'Henry, I want that £10 and I would appreciate it if you gave it back now. You are not well, Henry, but I am certain you could write a signed note confirming you owe me £10, or I can write it and you sign it!'

As Henry again sighed, I decided to take the bull by the horns and began rummaging through the drawers of a white clothing cabinet. Whilst doing so I angrily said, 'I'm looking for my money, Henry!' Without success, I continued the search, by checking the pockets of his trousers and jacket, which were hanging close by. I then sat back down on the visitors' chair and blasted, 'It would be easier to find the Lost City of Atlantis than my £10!'

I was interrupted from administering Henry with another 'piece of my mind' when a doctor in his mid-fifties entered the room; I took a few steps back from Henry's bed. 'What is the meaning of this? My patient is extremely weak. It is imperative he remains calm. He is not out of danger,' said the well-groomed and immaculately dressed doctor in a cultured yet authoritative manner.

'Your patient owes me £10. It is imperative he returns it!' I replied, attempting equal authority.

'Yes. You have made it noticeably clear how imperative

it is! Now grow up, man. Your friend is most poorly. If you cannot behave reasonably, I insist you leave.'

What an extremely rude doctor, I thought. *Telling such a distinguished scientist to grow up. Who does he think he is? The jumped-up twit!* Anyway, I held my tongue whilst the doctor settled him, glared at me and left the room. Immediately, Henry opened his eyes and said, 'Crawford, beware of feisty women. Strong, feisty women beware. They wore animal skins. They were like cave girls! Cave girls did this to me.'

Oh dear, I thought. *Just when I thought I could talk to him about my £10, he's become a gibbering idiot.* However, I attempted to reassure him. 'Pull yourself together, my friend; you've had an accident. You were injured in a road accident, a car crash… something like that.'

'This was no accident,' mumbled Henry. 'I was attacked. They were killing people. Thousands of people at our gig. The huge one I told you we were having. Our biggest ever gig. It was terrible. They were killing us all. All the crowd and all my mates in the band. My friends are now dead. I pretended I was too, and she forgot to stamp on my head. That is why I am alive. The police told me I was knocked down by a car when I was walking across a road, but I know that is not true. Look at me now, Crawford: they've told me here at the hospital that my body is so irreparably damaged that I may only have hours to live.' Henry was clearly physically exhausted and began coughing up fresh blood. I then noticed blood was now streaming from his ears. He was struggling so much now with his speech, but I managed to decipher, 'Help, get me the doctor, I can't breathe,' and he frantically reached for the emergency cord. I tied it up out of his reach and unplugged his life support machine so he would not be distracted by all those beeps, which had suddenly gone into frenzy.

'Don't worry about all that, Henry, the last thing we need in here is that stupid doctor. Tell me more about what happened. It's extremely exciting. I wish something like that would happen to me!' I enthused.

'Crawford...'

'Yes, go on, Henry.'

'Are you really a professor? Are you really a scientist?' groaned Henry.

'Yes. You know I am and a most brilliant one at that. What made you ask that?'

The hospital floor had now turned red with Henry's blood, which was now leaking from every orifice. Through a coughing fit Henry murmured, 'I just wondered how you achieved it.'

The rude doctor re-entered the room with two nurses. I considered it disrespectful of them to be putting his life support machine back on and replacing the emergency cord within Henry's reach. Surely a simple 'Is that ok with you, Professor Bond?' would have been nice! And why are you doing everything so fast as if it is an emergency? Henry is not royalty. He is just Henry. I was now getting angry. The staff were pretending I wasn't there. They do not even look at me. 'Excuse me! Excuse me!' As this was ignored, I said crossly, 'Anybody care to answer me? Hello!'

The doctor barked, 'Visiting time is over. You will leave the building now!'

'I will be filing a formal complaint about you, doctor.

You are here to make people better. Not to be rude. I am sure the General Medical Council will be extremely interested when they hear about this little episode. What is your name, Junior Doctor…?'

'Mr Dipsleek,' he said.

'So, you're not even a doctor!' I exclaimed.

'I am very much a doctor. I am a senior consultant. Visiting time is finished. I thought I had made that clear. Goodbye.'

'Well, Mr Pipsqueak, I don't see why I should leave this hospital until Henry makes arrangements for the return of my £10,' I protested.

The bemused consultant began shaking his head and started, 'In all the years of medical practice…' At the same time, he removed his own wallet from his pinstriped suit jacket and passed me a crisp £20 note. 'Take it. Do not worry about the change but don't come back. Oh, my name is Dipsleek, not Pipsqueak. I changed it many years ago by deed poll when I first became a doctor!'

I took the note and replied with a withering look. 'My friend is practically at death's door and you are concerned about £10? What is the world coming to?' With the medical team looking at each other, I turned on my heel and headed for the exit.

CHAPTER TWO
THE COVER-UP

Realising on my drive back from the hospital that I had very little information with which to piece together what had truly happened to Henry, I concluded that I should do what I always do when challenged with limited or conflicting data. So, using the car cassette player, I listened to the 1981 hit single *Einstein a Go-Go* by Landscape. Nodding my head and tapping my fingers on the steering wheel in rhythm, I sang along to the lyrics. I thought, *this will surely get my forensic science juices flowing!* 'You better watch out, you better beware, Albert said that E equals M C squared. Einstein a go-go. Einstein a go-go. Einstein a go-go…'

It had been quite a while since I had last seen my Barnsley home and I knew my neighbours would not have missed me. I was originally from Surrey and my current neighbours did not appreciate it when I felt the need to provide them all with elocution lessons every time we spoke. I experienced the same difficulties with my neighbours whilst living in Birmingham, Cardiff and Newcastle. As I walked along the path towards the front door, I was pleased to see that no vandals had mistaken my house for someone else's. Last time I returned, I had discovered 'weirdo freak' daubed on the outside of my front door.

I began my enquiries by telephoning Henry's parents,

who were to hang up each time they realised it was me. I can only imagine this had something to do with when I neglected to seek their permission to use their eighteenth-century grade II listed barn for a children's science television programme to illustrate that wood is more flammable than water. Next port of call were the boys in blue. I used to train their scenes of crime officers, so they would be helpful. Or so I thought.

'Why do you keep chuckling?' I asked angrily.

'I'm sorry,' Police Sergeant Tomlinson spouted, now almost crying with laughter. 'It's just that my wife is a nurse at the hospital, and you thought Henry Teague was the vacuum cleaner. Ha! No, it's all quite straightforward, run over by a car which failed to stop, sir. It's all in the file.'

'That's not what Henry has told me, Sergeant.'

'Vacuum cleaner, eh? We've investigated it thoroughly. We didn't let the dust settle. Ha ha. Unfortunately, we had no leads, unlike your mate. Ha, get it? I've got a million of them. Looking at his record, it doesn't look like he's ever had any brushes with the law. Ha ha, boom boom! Does he have a wife?'

'No,' I replied wearily.

'So, it's not time to change the old bag yet! Oh, on a serious note, though: the accident scene cleaned up nicely. Ha!'

'Very funny, Sergeant. I can see how you got your promotion.'

'Just before you leave, can I just ask you to keep a lookout when you're on your travels?' Sergeant Tomlinson pointed to a wall behind me with photographs of people. As I studied the ones headed 'MOST WANTED', he corrected my gaze. 'No, not those. This one.' I followed his finger until it landed on a poster that displayed a photograph of a tabby cat with 'MISSING' in bold text next to it. 'Toby is our biggest case right now. All police leave is cancelled until he's found. INTERPOL thought they had located him in Barcelona, but it was a different cat.'

I began walking away from the front desk of Rotheridge Police Station, and as I took a final glance at Toby, my peripheral vision showed me Sergeant Tomlinson was moving to an area behind the front desk office, an area intended to be out of sight from the public. I stopped when I heard the voice of a younger officer say, 'Sarge, we've got another one on the phone, wanting to report a missing person from that T. Rex tribute band concert at Rother Varley Country Park. Are we still telling them the same thing?'

'Yes, of course we are!' I heard PS Tomlinson snap. 'Take the details, tell them not to worry and that we will look into it but talk as much as you can about Toby the cat. Hopefully, everyone will be so busy looking for the cat they will forget about everything else. DCI Hughes has managed to sort out the press. That cat will dominate the news for as long as necessary.'

I knew there must be something fishy going on and the police were trying to conceal something. My suspicions deepened when I switched on the television to see full-length interviews with Toby's owners being broadcast on every TV channel, as well as press conferences led by the chief constable, flanked by other 'top brass', urging the entire nation to check sheds and outbuildings!

Gathering the evidence is what was needed, and I

started with extracting a trace of Henry's blood that had been on the hospital ward floor and transferred it to a piece of chewing gum stuck to the sole of my right shoe. This I transferred to a Petri dish in my home laboratory before heading to Rother Varley Country Park. There had clearly been a major clear-up operation as everything looked neat and tidy. Too tidy, in fact. Not a single item of litter. Undeterred, I took several photographs and measurements and took soil samples. I took stock of the entire location. There were no buildings in the vicinity so no chance of witnesses in that department. However, I did see that there were two horses in an adjoining field. For now, I thought, I have enough to get started.

Arriving back home I saw the newspaper had been delivered and I glanced at the headline:

'LEEDS UNITED STARS STOP TRAINING TO SEARCH FOR TOBY.'

The front page continued with how police chiefs right across the country were demanding that all businesses and schools must close and that it is the duty of every man, woman and child to find Toby the cat; the police were seeking emergency powers from the government to enforce the measure.

What on Earth had Henry got himself into? I must return to that hospital. On second thoughts, I didn't want to have to face Pipsqueak again. Back in my lab, the painstaking task of identifying valuable evidence from all other material began. In layman's terms, I was particularly interested in blood and any brain matter and fortunately, I had collected enough for my experiment. I would use a technique that I had perfected during a visit to a remote village in Tanzania. I had the foresight to leave Tanzania with several hundred litres of the required urine from chimpanzees who had drunk sap from the kigelia tree (also known as the sausage tree).

It was important to identify particles from the hippocampus (a part of the brain concerned with memory function). I added Henry's blood to the other blood samples, which were then coated on the brain particles. These were added to half a litre of urine and heated to thirty degrees Celsius. Once cooled to twenty-two degrees Celsius the liquid is dried onto a plastic tray in horizontal lines at a precise speed, theoretically, it may be possible for me to capture images of the most dramatic events in the lives of those persons from whom the brain particles came. It was entirely by fluke that the world's first Trippier 908 synthesiser was spawned some years previously. When connected to a compatible cathode-ray tube, (a component in a television or computer monitor) the most breath-taking visual images are reproduced on screen and from speakers. It is quite amazing how in science and medicine, significant breakthroughs transpire inadvertently. Between you and me, when I invented the Trippier 908, I was applying the finishing touches to an Airfix model aeroplane I was making. To say my aircraft went wrong would be a gross understatement! Inadvertently, I had spawned the world's first Trippier 908 synthesiser. When connected to a compatible cathode-ray tube, (a television set or computer monitor component) the most breath-taking visual images and sound are reproduced on screen and from speakers. However, payment I received from various Hollywood-based special effects teams, has ensured that the Trippier

908 remains off the market. Now, was my very own device still functional?

Theory had come up trumps. My experiment had worked to perfection. Henry was right. The gig had been hijacked by women looking like cave girls. Sure, they were strong, violent murderers who made a hell of a mess, but if you can see past all that, they also provided a great deal of pleasure for a great number of people. I watched it repeatedly for hours, dancing and partying to the music like a free-spirited youth!

I have never taken for granted just how privileged I have been during my long scientific career. My extensive travels have allowed me to explore in detail every region of the planet. I have been paid handsomely and my research generously funded, enough to meet all my requirements. Much of my vast knowledge has been passed to me by some of the people I have met. One such person is Texan horse breeder Bill Wade. Bill taught me the art of horse whispering and with a little practice, I became proficient.

The day after conducting the experiments that had enabled me to watch and listen to Skylie and the Pussycat Trolls, I decided to return to Henry's T. Rex concert venue. It took longer to get there than I expected due to the number of people using the roads. It seemed everyone was out. All the pavements were crowded, and I could see people looking under parked cars, searching front gardens and opening the rear doors of vans etc. Through my car window I heard the voices of both the old and the young calling, 'Toby! Toby! Where are you?' The authorities had successfully brainwashed the public and it was not long before the police stopped me to search my car for the 'missing cat'. After this I was unable to drive for more than half a mile before organised teams of the public, wearing yellow, hi-vis jackets stood in front of my Range Rover, as well as all other motor vehicles, to conduct further searches.

Eventually I arrived. The park was much busier than on my last visit, with well-intentioned citizens leaving no stone unturned in the desperate search for the famous feline. There they were, the fine 16.3 hand, chestnut, thoroughbred gelding and his little, grey, Welsh cob mate, grazing on the grass in the same field as last time. I approached them as calmly as I could but both equines lifted their heads, and as I saw their big, brown, suspicious eyes descend on me, the munching stopped. The small cob asked, 'What's new, pussycat?'

I explained the purpose of my visit, to which the thoroughbred said to me with his upper-class accent, 'Can't help you, old boy, with that one. We didn't see a damn sausage. Cheerio.' As both horses began to walk away, I tried a different tack.

I enquired, 'How about you, short arse?'

The little fella stopped dead and faced me. 'No need to be rude boyo,' he replied with such a distinctive accent, it was just liking speaking to Sir Tom Jones. Goodness gracious me, even his mannerisms and facial expressions were spot on. I concluded that he must share some of the same genes. But a sweaty, rounded and stubby little double of Tom Jones, covered head to toe with flies... It's not unusual!

Now showing a bag of fresh carrots, I said, 'Are you quite sure you didn't see anything?'

'Well, now. Let me think. I do recall something at the

T. Rex concert. There was a big commotion when some cave girls turned up.'

My supermarket bag emptied as I tried concentrating on the account whilst spending equal time correcting any of his mispronunciations, but at least now I had heard it from 'the horse's mouth'. The carrots had done the trick. It is remarkable how observant horses can be. The cob provided a detailed and comprehensive narrative and even began dancing as he described the choreography of the women's act. Eventually I draw the conversation to a close but told the small horse he should not apologise after he said, 'I'm sorry if I ramble on a bit; other horses are always telling me I talk the hind legs off a donkey!'

As I slowly walked towards my large four-wheel drive, I was thinking how nice it was to have a good old horse whispering session again. However, darker thoughts were about to enter my mind. The public had been brainwashed. The police had been seeking draconian powers through emergency legislation. There has been a complete news blackout regarding Henry's T. Rex tribute act. Who can I turn to about what I have discovered? There is certainly a high-level cover-up, so is it safe for me to speak out? I decided that I needed 'a bit of me time' alone in the laboratory, to savour a glass of red wine whilst listening to the cracking tunes of Skylie and the Pussycat Trolls. However, a shudder was about to run down my spine: I looked back at the field where I had been horse whispering. There, having a full-blown chat with the cob himself, was a black, Irish, draught, thoroughbred cross, police horse with an officer on its back. That police horse did not look as if it was looking for a lost moggy! The two horses nodded and shook their heads in natter but when I saw the cob wink at the police horse, I had the distinct feeling that the little short arse had just grassed me up. Especially when the policeman gave him an apple!

I am usually calm at home but on this occasion I felt nervous and apprehensive. Having been in the property for about ten minutes, I started to fill the kettle, but my anxiety heightened upon hearing a loud knocking on the front door. It was certainly no surprise when I saw two male police officers as I pulled the door open. To cut a long story short, the Welsh cob's name was 'Little Snitch' and he was a police informer who passed them information in exchange for apples. Parliament had passed the emergency legislation and the police, now armed with special new powers, were arresting me 'for failing to search for Toby' contrary to Section 2 of the Missing Toby Bill, Emergency Powers Act 1920.

As the police car had now been travelling south along the M1 for over an hour, I enquired, 'Shouldn't we be at the police station by now?'

'Just relax, Professor. We are not local officers. We are from the Metropolitan Police in London and we've been instructed to take you to the capital. You will be provided with a meal and someone there will speak to you.' It was apparent this was no ordinary arrest, and on completion of the journey, I was not at any police station. I was led by police into a government building, the Ministry of Defence Main Building, Whitehall, London SW1, to be precise. I was not handcuffed but handed over to a clean-shaven male, Sam, in his twenties wearing a slightly ill-fitting charcoal-coloured suit. Sam escorted me into a canteen and he stayed with me while I consumed a meal. I was no longer apprehensive. Sam was friendly but said little at this time. After my adequate meal, he took me into the basement area and said to me, 'Unofficially, we refer to this part of the building as "Pindar". Pindar was an ancient Greek poet and I'm not certain why we call it that. Officially, it is the Defence Crisis Management Centre.'

We walked together through a series of corridors until one opened into an enormous hall with a row of individual black-seated chairs. 'No one will be available to speak to you today, but all will be revealed tomorrow. I'm going to make sure your room has been prepared as you will be required to sleep here tonight. I will leave you here for a few minutes but be prepared for some colleagues of mine to introduce themselves to you.'

All I could muster was a feeble 'okay'. I didn't know what else to say. This was all very sinister 'cloak and dagger' stuff, yet also immensely intriguing. I sat on a chair in the middle of the row while Sam left me. As I admired my surroundings, I didn't take note of Sam's direction of departure; it was as if he just vanished. The hall consisted of thick, wood-panelled walls and ceiling and six very wide, magnificent and regal-looking oak doors. Yet, rather than being the least bit dingy, the area was well illuminated and bright. Simultaneously, the six doors opened, and from each a woman entered the hall and stood before me.

Not being able to put my finger on what was not quite right about these smiling and attractive women, I gazed a little deeper. Was it their hair? No, it was not that. All possessed nice figures and appeared well-toned. So, what was it? As my eyes looked them up and down, the smallest one said to me, 'Everything is where it should be.' Only one thing now mattered. The accent! I need to iron out that intonation.

'You're Australian!' I blasted.

A dark-haired woman began to laugh and said, 'What a silly-looking, little man, he is.'

'An American accent! Is speaking in the Queen's English too much to ask?' At the four other girls, I continued, 'I would like to hear the rest of you speak. Please restore my faith that my beautiful mother tongue may be delivered as intended.'

All six girls shrieked in uncontrollable laughter but the body language of one woman with red hair was aggressive and she moved menacingly towards me. The one with dark hair intervened. 'No, Sarmit. Leave him.'

'I don't like him, Nicola,' said red-headed Sarmit with that awful twang from across the pond!

As Sarmit grudgingly moved back to where she had originally been standing, the small blonde with the Australian accent said, 'I vote we give him a chance. He probably needs to have a bit of fun and loosen up a bit!'

'As always, Skylie, you are right. We will give him a chance,' said Nicola, seemingly to me to be in control of the other women.

In the pause that followed, I reflected on what it was that I had thought odd about these women. They were all barefooted. Perfectly reasonable, I concluded. They were all dressed in animal skins, which seemed normal to me. Their jewellery was made from large, sharp-pointed teeth and they all carried large clubs. Nothing unusual so far. Then the eureka moment: those live, fully-grown African bull elephants carried effortlessly on each girl's back! I concluded only a learned professor would pay such attention to detail as to notice elephants and I congratulated myself on being so smart.

'How are you all getting on?' asked Sam, re-entering the hall.

'I'm at a loss as to what is going on here, Sam. Please tell me what it is. Do you wish to provide these women with elocution lessons?' I asked.

'All will be revealed tomorrow,' replied Sam. 'Elocution lessons. Elocution lessons,' he added, chuckling away to himself. The ladies then exited the hall but this time they all used the same door. I was shown to an individual bedroom, where I surprisingly slept most soundly.

CHAPTER THREE
REVELATIONS

After breakfast the following morning, Sam led me to a conference room and sat me down at a large table. I found myself directly facing the British prime minster, Mrs Margaret Thatcher, Home Secretary Leon Brittan, Field Marshall Sir Edwin Bramall (head of the British armed forces) and Sir Kenneth Newman (commissioner of the Metropolitan Police Service). Sam sat at a chair at the back of the room.

Mrs Thatcher looked at me and said, 'I do not know if you have met any of us previously but I am certain that introductions will not be necessary, so I will cut to the chase. I am wishing to avert a global emergency, Professor.'

'By arresting me for not looking for a cat?' I drily replied.

Ignoring my sarcasm, she continued, 'Professor of Public Engagement at the University of Washington, a PHD in paleopathology, a PHD in palaeontology, physical anthropologist as well as a biological anthropologist. You are indeed a clever man.'

'A genius, actually,' I said, now sensing that her flattery indicated they needed my help and I had the upper hand.

The prime minister's matter-of-fact demeanour became noticeably sterner. 'Yes, as well as intolerant, particularly with regional accents, rude, pedantic, childish and on occasions, incredibly unobservant. I am surprised you did not recognise those women you met yesterday,' she said.

'Why would I recognise them?' I puzzled.

'You miraculously discovered a way of being able to play back and witness the incident at your friend's event, yet failed to make a connection with the women you met yesterday. The elephants didn't even make the penny drop with you. I sometimes hear those elephants trumpeting when I'm in Downing Street. Those particular animals were deemed too aggressive to be kept in the zoo, no keeper would approach them. Yet they are submissive with the girls. They even perform squat thrusts with the elephants on their backs! Those are the girls who attacked your friend. As you left your equipment set up in your lab, we used it following your arrest and saw what you had been viewing. You met Skylie and the Pussycat Trolls yesterday. You are clever but you are also a buffoon! I mean, what kind of scientist produces a rocket-powered walking frame, then decides to release the residual nitrous oxide at a funeral wake? Only you, Bond! That said, we need your assistance,' said Mrs Thatcher.

I had barely glanced at the other people in the room but almost felt them leaning in closer towards me.

'And if I decline?' I asked.

Sir Kenneth Newman chipped in with, 'If you refuse to help the UK government, you will be charged with not searching for Toby the cat. You will never be seen again; you will vanish off the face of the world and the public will be only too delighted when told you had been given a life sentence. Is that clear enough, Bond?'

The self-satisfied facial expression displayed on the face of the police chief soon disappeared, as Mrs Thatcher referred to the 1982 Steven Spielberg film and tore into him. 'Shut it, ET. Leave the talking to me. Hope that's clear enough, Newman!' As Sir Kenneth blushed, the PM addressed me. 'Now, Professor, we have a bit of a situation here. These women are known to us. In fact, they are a vital component in our national security. You will learn in due course why your friend and the rest of his group were attacked. We want you to work with these women. Officially they do not exist, yet certain foreign governments are aware of them.

'I don't wish to insult your intelligence, Professor, but for illustration purposes I would like you to imagine you are at home watching the news when the newscaster astonishingly reveals that your previous knowledge of natural history and evolution had been a deliberate attempt to conceal the truth. A bit like Toby the missing cat.

'You sit glued to the TV as the BBC explain to the nation that the dinosaurs were not wiped out because of ice ages or any giant meteor strikes. Each one was killed millions of years ago by members of a highly advanced, yet supremely aggressive female tribe called Cave Girls, or CGs. Since the dawn of time, they have possessed electronic devices superior to anything we have in place today. For example, they used portable telephones, which they called smart phones. These women are only called Cave Girls because they created caves for early man to live. Such is their extraordinary strength, they carved them out by hand. Anyway, these women set about committing the most savage slaughter of the dinosaurs simply because they became fed up with removing dinosaur faeces from the surrounding grounds of their stately mansions. We know from these ladies that one day, a primitive man emerged from his cave and made a series of grunts that translated as "Hey, dudes, what happened to all the dinosaurs?" Shockingly, but much later, the same female tribe went on to cause the demise of the dodo whilst on a spa weekend on the island of Mauritius!

'By and large these women remain under control but only because they choose so. At the present time, they are content to play second fiddle and let us take the lead. They even assist us, the government, when requested and as a matter of principle we pay them. They are superior to us in all departments and they find our feeble attempts to make the world work, highly amusing. Every now and then we are delivered a reminder of who is really in charge. Your friend's T. Rex tribute concert, for example. A more serious and permanent CG takeover will happen whenever these women decide. Such a situation acutely threatens all life on the planet, including human. I know you are not a layman, so please forgive me, but in layman's terms, these women carry Cave Girl DNA.

'You can help us, Professor, but more about that later. For now, please just listen to me. We know that CGs exist within the wider community; possibly she may be 'the girl next door', the woman serving in Tesco or the lovely and friendly lollipop lady, helping the children across the road. However, complacency on our part and we are left with the girl next door turning your entire street into a pile of rubble, the woman in Tesco crushing every baked bean tin in stock with just two fingers, and drivers and pedestrians fleeing for their lives, from the now-maniac lollipop lady who has just sliced a double-decker bus in half!

'CGs are a distinct breed, entirely separate from other *Homo sapiens*, and they have brutally influenced evolution and ancient history. These ladies decided about sixty-five million years ago, at the end of the Cretaceous Period, to wipe out the remaining dinosaurs on Earth. As I mentioned to you before, Crawford, they became fed up with the dinosaurs defecating on and trampling the lawns surrounding their fabulous homes. Not only did CGs live in luxurious accommodation; they drove high-end motor cars that they called SUVs, they used 'smart' telephones and they claim to have regularly embarked on internet shopping, whatever that is.

'The public are nowhere near ready for any of this to be revealed. The shock would no doubt result in terrible panic, which is why on the occasions where there has been a CG incident, it has been necessary for mass distraction plans to be put in place. Or, to put it another way, a cover-up. Toby the missing cat is such an example. The great British public's love of animals is most useful at times. The traditional, yet fabricated theories on natural history, have served governments well. Charles Darwin was paid a fortune to remove all references to Cave Girls from his works. Also, chauvinistic attitudes have played a vital role over the centuries. It did not happen by chance that, hundreds of years ago, the idea that women could at any time achieve world domination would have been so unpalatable that a mere mention would have resulted in a life of incarceration; those in authority deliberately portrayed the male as being the stronger sex to dispel rumours of a superior female race. The effects of ice ages and meteor strikes have been grossly exaggerated to suppress what really happened to the dinosaurs. As a matter of fact, it was women like Skylie and the Pussycat Trolls who sealed the fate of dinosaurs, as well as seventy per cent of all other life that existed at that time.'

I said, 'I never did fall for that Ice Age thing. I discovered too many lipstick-stained fag butts next to fossilised dinosaur remains during my expeditions.'

Mrs Thatcher nodded and went on. 'We knew you were getting remarkably close. These girls would often relax by smoking a cigarette after a kill. We were considering having you assassinated. Still are, actually. The thing is, Crawford, these CGs are highly unpredictable and, whilst they largely remain unnoticed, they are prone to biblical levels of violence and destruction. On discovering Henry's event up in Yorkshire, they probably assumed T. Rex to be an actual living tyrannosaurus and went into a combat mode. Once activated, the women's insatiable prey drive must be satisfied. Had Henry been the front man of an ABBA tribute act, all that carnage in Yorkshire would have been avoided.

'As you are aware, Professor, two hundred thousand years ago Neanderthal men were decorating the interiors of their caves with pictures of animals. Examples of these cave drawings are displayed in books and in museums, but we know you have made discoveries of your own, Crawford. Tell me about what you found during your excavations in Spain and southern Italy. Because, Crawford, you were not meant to find them.'

I replied, 'I take it you mean the sinister ones. The paintings that appear to have been created by talented artists, entirely different from all other cave paintings. The ones depicting women as being vastly superior to the men, in terms of both mental intellect and physical strength. The ones that illustrate a female tribe as being the dominant species, who attack dinosaurs while the men flee. Are these the ones you mean, Prime Minister?'

'Yes, of course I mean those ones, together with the others drawn millions of years ago showing the girls visiting hair and beauty salons, receiving manicures, pedicures and other treatments including tattoos. The government will introduce a scapegoat to further inconvenient art discoveries. He will be a shadowy, enigmatic figure who will, in the dead of night, leave graffiti on walls and buildings in prominent view. His work must often portray a satirical message as is to be considered street art. If we get this right, no one will ever see him at work, and will be guessing his actual identity for years. Branson, Bailey, Banksy. Voila! We will call him Banksy. If the public ever do see the paintings you discovered, Banksy will take full credit.'

'Mrs Thatcher, you mentioned something earlier about *Raphus cucullatus*, the dodo?'

'It was during a spa weekend in the year 1602 on the island of Mauritius, that six CGs first focussed their eyes on the dodo. These feathered creatures stood no chance as, in-between their pampering sessions, Betty and her friends dispatched each bird to the last. As incredible as it may seem, the world's entire population of 651,000 was wiped out by these six women in the space of four hours, fifty-three minutes and eighteen seconds! I can also reveal that in the year 1884, CGs' antics and love of leather left the American bison perilously close to extinction. For obvious reasons, we have always had to blame European settlers for persecuting the bison.

'Now, when people see a dead fox or badger in the gutter with guts and intestines dangling all over the place, people automatically assume the animal to be another roadkill victim. This is good as nobody asks any questions; however, it is equally likely to have become the quarry of a

CG. This is where you come in, Professor. We have many CGs on the payroll, as does the United States. Regrettably, the Soviet Union has some too and as these women are, in effect, weapons of mass destruction, we certainly don't want to escalate an arms race in which the Soviets begin to stockpile CGs for use against the West.' I glanced at Sir Edwin Bramall as he solemnly nodded in agreement with the PM. Mrs Thatcher continued, 'So we have taken the liberty of tendering your resignation from the University of Washington so that you are able to work for us without distraction. You should be flattered; we will double your previous salary and—'

'Just a minute. I will need to consider this. There is much for me to think about here,' I interrupted.

'I was about to say and £10. We will double your salary plus £10,' said Mrs Thatcher.

'Okay, I'm interested now.'

'Your predecessor, Professor Roger Knight, took early retirement. A couple of days before the T. Rex concert, Roger asked a CG to fetch him a genuine mug of Yorkshire tea. It appears she went to Yorkshire for it and took her friends along too. We all know what happened then. Roger felt it was the right time for him to go,' Mrs Thatcher continued. 'As you have been made aware, there are CGs existing within the public. Some working in supermarkets, whilst others may be dating Formula 1 racing drivers or featuring heavily on TV adverts for hair products and German branded yogurts, as well as being panel judges for televised talent shows. Your role will be one of research into CG behaviour, helping maintain harmony between humans and CGs, as well as identifying and recruiting more CGs in the interests of national security. You will be head of the CG Department; all your staff will have relevant scientific qualifications and experience. You will also have your own office and laboratory within Pindar. You will report directly to your line manager, Sir Edwin.'

A door suddenly burst open and Nicola walked in, dragging behind her a bright, post box red Sir Giles Gilbert Scott designed K6 version telephone kiosk. Impersonating Spielberg's character, she said, 'ET phone home.' She was clearly mocking Sir Kenneth. 'How you doing, Maggie?' Mrs Thatcher looked away and appeared slightly embarrassed. Then Nicola addressed me. 'You've got them all with you today, even Field Harvester Bramall and Fatty Brittan! Oh, yes, they love us CGs. Just remember: CG stands for Considerably Greater.'

I asked Nicola, 'Are you going to be difficult?'

Nicola then walked over to Sir Kenneth, who was looking particularly awkward and nervous. She leant over him and again said, 'ET phone home.' She then walked out of the door, taking the large telephone booth with her.

The prime minister said to me, 'I think that gives you your answer. This will be a challenging role.'

CHAPTER FOUR
TOP-SECRET INFORMATION

When I started my career as a senior government scientist, I had full access to all relevant data. All that relates to Cave Girls is classified as top secret. Working with these women would be far from easy but I knew that I could only be compared against Professor Knight and he had failed.

To you, the reader, I trust that you are blessed with sufficient maturity to receive the information that I shall impart, but if you are of a nervous disposition, you should refrain from reading any further. CGs seemed to have existed for as long as there has been life on Earth. It is not known how many CGs are in existence today but there is no evidence that they become ill or suffer the effects of ageing; there are no recorded CG deaths. The Cave Girls I have worked with have provided first-hand accounts from events spanning millions of years in history.

After reading the fascinating documents regarding the fall of the Roman Empire, I asked the particularly laid-back and friendly CG Natalie to confirm a few details. As the saying goes, 'Rome was not built in a day', but Natalie claimed CGs could actually build several Romes in a day. As it transpires, the whole city was built within three hours by a team of just six CG builders. Four hours after the foundations had been laid on a desolate, barren landscape, thousands of residents moved into quality housing. They were relaxing in the famous Roman baths and many were instantly earning a decent living with the intelligently laid infrastructure designed for economic growth.

Natalie told me that she particularly enjoyed building the Colosseum in AD 70. Her work was entirely handcrafted and took her twenty minutes to complete. She then lent a helping hand to the other women. She explained how it was such a shame that the Romans eventually 'became too big for their boots'. Natalie described it as an 'utter betrayal' when on 1st January 404 she entered the floor of the arena to retrieve her hair band, which had fallen from her head whilst she had been seated high up. At this precise time, four male gladiators with particularly fearsome reputations occupied the stage and were in combat in a 'champ of champs' fight to the death. According to Nat, some 'giggling nobility nerd' shouted 'Kill the cave girl'! Regarding this as an order, the gladiators immediately attacked the poor, unarmed woman. What a mistake this was to prove. Within a split second, the four previously undefeated champions lay slain, their throats having been slit with their own weapons.

As other gladiators fell as quickly as they could enter the arena, Roman centurions were summoned to restore order. However, with Natalie now well and truly in full flow and with the city's soldiers having become corpses, lions, tigers and bears were released on Natalie in one final attempt to quell the emergency. Ultimately, this was to be in vain as each powerful beast was decapitated. With the panicked spectators scrambling for the exits, many were to die from crush injuries caused by the weight of thousands of other human beings stepping or crawling over them.

With the carnage almost complete, the CG punched

through the Colosseum's thick walls and exited the vast sporting venue. As the bewildered citizens of Rome stumbled along the streets, Natalie stamped her foot, which caused a 9.0 earthquake and any remaining souls were killed by falling masonry and the once-mighty Rome fell in spectacular fashion. All that was left to do now was for Natalie to message some old CG pals for a get-together and chinwag, whilst they drank the gallons of wine stored in underground vaults. Natalie explained how other ancient cities had been built by CG friends of hers, and under the guidance of these women, the ancient civilisations of, for example, Greece and China had flourished. She told me how Rome had later been rebuilt without CG involvement and consequently with inferior workmanship. 'Had I rebuilt the Colosseum myself, it would still look like new, instead of that dilapidated, crumbling monstrosity we see today.' Something that constantly struck me about Nat is just how natural and unassuming she always was. I am delighted to say we remain in contact and she never fails to send me a birthday card.

In World War Two, Adolf Hitler's Nazi forces fiercely battled the army of the Soviet Union. Elite German stormtroopers had, with relative ease, advanced deep into the vast Communist country. However, on 2nd February 1943, the tide was to turn heavily in favour of the Red Army. CG Mila sat in my office and laughed as I read her file. As I looked up at her, Mila said, 'Not bad going for a little woman like me.' It turned out that Joseph Stalin, the Russian head of state, had at last decided to play his trump card: Mila, the only known CG behind the Iron Curtain during the war. On receiving orders to engage, this Cave

Girl was the decisive factor of the Battle of Stalingrad. She single-handedly took control of the city of Stalingrad (now Volgograd). In just one hour, she achieved more than most nations do in years of conflict. Mila's sixty-minute Cave Girl rampage ensured that not a single German soldier remained alive within the Soviet Union. Senior Private Herman Schmidt was the only German to survive. He had been one of the first to be attacked, and Mila had taken hold of him by the throat, before throwing him high up over the clouds and back into Germany, which was over a thousand miles away. Schmidt was able to swim to safety after falling into Lake Constance. Had he remained in the water a further ten seconds, Schmidt would have been struck by a German Tiger II tank that Mila had also propelled across the sky! With the Soviet CG having eradicated Hitler's forces, Mila continued her advance, now pushing the retreating German Army out of Poland. The 'little woman' was even responsible for downing over a hundred enemy aircraft, achieved by throwing debris from the ground at them. Mila's effectiveness in battle was starting to cause some disquiet among Allied leaders, so, with this in mind, Stalin took the decision to recall Mila, who had advanced as far as Berlin in just one day! At the end of World War Two, Mila moved to London and for a time, ran a tearoom.

When reading another file, I was shocked at the appalling level of deceit that the UK government and other British institutions would go to suppress the truth from the public. Within the file was a witness statement that had been taken by police in a London hospital following the 1981 Brixton Riots. The witness admitted that he had been unlawfully active within the disorders: 'I know we did some pretty bad things, throwing bricks and petrol bombs and all that. We were winning until those Cave Girl things got out of a police riot van and they began smashing us up. One of my friends is now a vegetable. I know the police wanted to stop all that rioting but Cave Girls? We didn't deserve that!'

I can confirm that compensation has been paid out to the victims and their families. However, the file made clear that law enforcement agencies both here and overseas deployed CGs to quell large-scale public disorder on the streets, within prisons and even on military operations. The use of CGs during the 1981 Brixton Riots was far from being an isolated case. In 2014, a public announcement was going to be made during an arranged press conference and live television broadcast where the assistant commissioner would declare, 'On behalf of the Metropolitan Police and all other police services across England and Wales, I wish to apologise unreservedly for the deployment of Cave Girls. The scale of public disorder during the incidents that we refer to as the 1981 Brixton Riots was unprecedented and our officers had been subject to violent and sustained attacks. This unacceptable behaviour involved police officers being deliberately targeted with petrol bombs and other weapons. Regardless of what I have just said, the use of Cave Girls as a means to restore order was totally disproportionate and it is unfortunate as well as undefendable, that the Metropolitan Police Service, together with other forces, decided until now to conceal and even deny the fact that Cave Girls had been utilised by the police during the 1981 Brixton Riots and on other occasions across the UK. To make this absolutely clear, this is an unreserved apology, and although money alone will not make matters right, we are in the process of implementing a compensation scheme. At present the total value of the arrangement stands at £58 million but will be under constant review as to whether this amount is sufficient. The life-changing injuries that occurred at the hands of these Cave Girls, as well as the long-term suffering experienced not just by the victims but also their families, friends and loved ones, are fully acknowledged. This must never be forgotten. Policy and safeguarding changes are now in place to ensure that nothing of this nature is ever repeated.'

The press conference was cancelled and the apology was never made. Prime Minister David Cameron ordered a total news blackout and he succeeded in keeping CGs out of the public domain. Although governments generally abide by an unwritten rule in the Geneva Convention that 'wide use of CGs is prohibited', the secrecy surrounding the issue does effectively allow states free rein regarding the use of these women. I find this very unsatisfactory; after all, these women are internationally classified as WMDs (weapons of mass destruction)!

CHAPTER FIVE
THE GREATS AND THE NOT-SO GREATS

Being the world's leading authority on CGs, my work was regularly interrupted by various heads of state telephoning me for advice on CG issues. President Vladimir Putin seemed to have more challenges with CGs than most and was experiencing teething issues within his own, newly formed, Tactical CG Unit. I clearly remember one day, in August 2016, asking CG Catherine to assist in translating part of one of his questions. When I asked her how she had such detailed knowledge of 'all things Russian', Catherine revealed that she was in fact Catherine the Great!

So, before me stood a true 'great', the architect of the 'Catherine Era'. She oversaw Russia's golden age. Not only did she modernise Russia; she also increased its original size by 200,000 square miles and ensured that the country was established as a world superpower. However, she confided in me that she found being so much in the public gaze 'restrictive', so she ensured that legal documents be produced that would record that she had died on 17th November 1796.

Hopefully, Catherine will not be too angry if I reveal a little more. After her 'passing', she travelled to Italy and busied herself designing their modern national flag. From a small room in an abandoned windmill, this woman handmade and distributed her products on an industrial scale. On 7th January 1797, in her first hour of production, she managed to make more flags than the number of flags that exist in the world today. It was probably a good thing Catherine did design the Italian flag because the country's one-time chief flag designer, Luigi Russo, was proposing a design featuring a Margherita pizza!

Catherine decided to explore and it was just six days later that nine hundred French seamen were killed, when their vessel was lifted from the Mediterranean waters and hurled half a mile before Catherine capsized the hull with the palm of her hand. Officially, the ship was a casualty of the French Revolutionary Wars. In truth, CG Catherine had become disgusted witnessing its French captain picking his nose and flicking dried nasal mucus into the water!

This woman continued swimming until reaching Ecuador on 4th February 1797. As she walked across dry land, she was pestered by a wasp. However, when she managed to stamp on the insect, this was to result in the 'Riobamba Earthquake', which claimed the lives of 40,000 people. Deciding it was a good time to leave, Catherine swam from the Americas to the coast of Portugal. Here, Catherine provided tactical guidance to Admiral Sir John Jervis and Commodore Horatio Nelson of the Royal Navy. Her words of wisdom proved a key turning point during the Battle of Cape St Vincent, which became a decisive British victory on 14th February 1797.

The mighty athlete made light work crossing the thousands of miles of ocean separating Europe and the Caribbean, completing the swim in under ninety minutes. This was to leave her plenty of time to make several electric fridge/freezers, which she introduced to the locals while also serving them banana splits. After this she 'took her seat' and watched the British invasion of Trinidad on 18th February 1797. The Brits were led by Sir Ralph Abercromby, who was commanding a fleet of eighteen warships. Trinidad was under Spanish control, and although Catherine had only intended to be a spectator, the island's governor, Don José Maria Chacón, spotted Catherine and rightly suspected her of being a CG. The Spaniard immediately surrendered the island to Catherine, who passed control to Abercromby. A large quantity of refreshing ice cream was then enjoyed and even the Spanish were permitted to lick the scrapings!

One day later, Catherine was in Wales and for the first time saw Colonel William Tate, who was, in her words, 'That silly little twerp'. Tate was particularly hostile towards Britain and he had landed near Fishguard with a French military unit that was 1,400 men strong. The unit was known as 'La Légion Noire' (The Black Legion). Tate's landing would be dubbed 'The Last Invasion of Britain'.

The CG followed his antics with mild amusement for three days before choosing to halt his progress. On 22nd February 1797, Catherine stood directly in front of Tate and verbally humiliated him. Tate's fearsome reputation was in tatters as the woman poked fun at him and told his men 'William Tate jokes'. Members of his legendary elite military unit suddenly lost all discipline as they rolled around in laughter. Catherine's Cave Girl wit was so sharp that Tate's men began to experience involuntary muscle spasms, leading to the accidental discharge of their firearms. Consequently, ninety-three per cent of Tate's unit perished in friendly fire.

Paris is worth a visit at any time of the year, and the

former empress paid the city a visit on 22nd October 1797 to see André-Jacques Garnerin attempt the world's first ever parachute jump over the city from a hydrogen balloon. On his first attempt, the parachute failed to open but Catherine saved him from a certain death as he plummeted at 120 m.p.h. Standing beneath him, she managed to catch him and gently lowered him to the ground. Although the Frenchman's second attempt was more promising, he had neglected to consider an air vent in the design, which resulted in the parachute being difficult and dangerous to control.

Catherine modified his equipment so that it operated perfectly. She then provided entertainment of her own to the large crowd by practising hundreds of parachute jumps from over 800 metres, which she managed without the aid of any type of aircraft or platform!

Now, let us compare Catherine the Great with King Alfred the Great. Born at Wantage, Berkshire, in AD 849, King Alfred is one of the outstanding figures in English history. Noted for his military successes against Viking forces, Alfred is the only English monarch known as 'great'. Yet, according to Skylie, 'He was highly overrated'. She should know; he burned her cakes!

Every CG account is scientifically verified. I have been able to prove beyond doubt that whatever any CG has told me is a hundred per cent accurate. King Alfred has been credited with several military victories. All these victories were in fact won by CG Skylie. In AD 871, Skylie attacked the ferocious Viking invaders in the Battle of Ashdown, until their leader, Guthrum, pleaded with her to stop killing his men. Whilst this had been going on, Alfred had been hiding in a cave that Skylie had made for him.

Skylie, who was Alfred's personal bodyguard, advised the king to lie low in the Somerset Marshes whilst she hunted Vikings. Finally, in AD 878, apart from Guthrum, the invaders were exterminated during one of Skylie's infamous 'spinning around' routines. As the Viking leader was now stranded in England, Skylie suggested he become friends with Alfred and the pair got on so well that Guthrum was to become Alfred's adoptive son. I am sorry to say that the popular folklore tale regarding Alfred's burning of the cakes is yet another example of how history has been grotesquely distorted to deny the existence of CGs. In fact, Skylie was showing Alfred the art of cake making and when he tried his hand, there was a complete disaster!

In Winchester there is a fine statue of King Alfred the Great. This was designed by Hamo Thornycroft R.A. and erected in 1899 to mark one thousand years since Alfred's death. Previously, a statue of Skylie had stood within the city; however, her statue was removed when people asked probing questions regarding her apparent 'superhero' capabilities.

CHAPTER SIX
THE CAVE GIRL BUILDERS

CGs are extremely expensive for any government. Although no details will be officially published, each year just one CG will cost the equivalent of the entire NHS budget. My department was heavily involved in research and in keeping CGs stimulated. Most importantly, CGs must be content, even if it means awarding them extremely high salaries. The future of humanity depends on these women. If we alienate them, we will vanish as suddenly as the dinosaurs did. CGs are occasionally tasked with security and government close-protection work. In 1995, I oversaw an experiment in which all police officers within the Greater Manchester policing district were placed on leave for a period of thirty consecutive days. CG Nicola was drafted to Manchester to replace the police during this period. The experiment was a partial success in that all the city's criminals were behind bars within day one. For the remainder of the month, Manchester remained crime-free and was statistically the safest location on the planet. On the downside, there was a disproportionate number of deaths in custody. One prisoner complained to her about the cells being overcrowded so Nicola immediately initiated a fast-track process of court trials, yet held within the police station, with her assuming the positions of both judge and jury. All prisoners were found guilty and most were sentenced to death.

Due to the immense costs of keeping CGs, the UK government has always sought ways in which these women can generate revenue. One of my roles was to source work for them in the UK and overseas. Orders for building and construction projects were the most usual. The obvious difficulty was emphasising the girls' effectiveness to boost sales, while concealing the existence from the public. The UK government has, in general, compromised secrecy for commercial interests by revealing the CGs' existence to a select few. These few are typically the heads of state and senior politicians of the world's wealthiest nations, royal families, and certain celebrities.

Those rich and privileged enough to hire a CG builder will witness building construction that is in a different league and light years away from the construction methods of even the finest of other master builders. These girls are extremely flexible with regard to their work. No job is too small or too large. Equal skill and care will be demonstrated if assembling a single piece of flat-pack furniture or a major city. All builds are of flawless quality, made without the use of any tools, yet completed at incredible speed.

In providing that essential 'Cave Girl touch', these women draw on the wealth of knowledge and experience that others can only envy. Remember that 100,000 years ago, the girls were carving out caves for early man to live in. A few chosen men were able to enjoy electric lighting and central heating. However, these women have always had for themselves the most opulent abodes imaginable. CGs have always been at the forefront of innovation. Cities they crafted thousands of years ago, all included a host of world-class entertainment facilities, including casinos and nightclubs equipped with the most advanced 'smart' technology.

I have accompanied CGs to parts of the developing world and witnessed their monumental achievements. Within a few short hours, deserts have been transformed into unlimited housing for all social groups; hospitals, schools, places of worship and magnificent multipurpose stadiums have been in place. Light and heavy industrial units have also been included where necessary. Power is sourced from clean, renewable energy and the very highest global green rating scores are always met. Congested roads, poor rail links, pollution, flooding and all other inherent and unwelcome issues that typify the work of others do not prevail in a CG city, owing to a piece of ingenious technology known only to these women. When Tony Blair held the office of prime minister, he stated within internal documents, 'The cities designed and built by Cave Girl Builders are quite frankly a joy to live and work in. They will provide the foundations for increasing strength within any economy and, as a Cave Girl city is a "must visit city", vital revenue will be generated by means of tourism, trade and local enterprise. Personally, I would like to see the whole of the UK redesigned by the girls.' I remember how impressed Tony had been when I showed him a letter that had been written by a prominent historical figure. Part of the letter read, 'I was asked by the British government to rebuild London following that dreadful fire. I had not the faintest idea as to where to start. Luckily, a Cave Girl did it for me and at such amazing speed. She had St Paul's Cathedral splendidly erected in eight minutes and twenty seconds'. (Signed Sir Christopher Wren 1711).

It says something of the modesty of CGs that they are content to let others take the credit for their achievements. So, I will tell you now that CGs designed and built all the Pyramids in Egypt, the Luxor Temple, the Temple of Hera and the Great Wall of China. When it comes to constructing major developments and cities within hours, a CG would be the only choice for a government. Working with CGs provided the personal benefit for me of having my investment portfolio properties, fully furnished with flat-pack furniture, assembled in milliseconds!

King David I was understandably proud of the Scottish city of Edinburgh, which was built by CG Katy in the twelfth century. King David said, 'My goodness, what a splendid job Katy has made. Such fine work. She built the city in a jiffy. I do like the castle. It's like the sandcastles my mummy made for me on the beach!' More recent times have seen the emergence of skyscrapers. At 2,717ft, the Burj Khalifa in Dubai remains the world's tallest building. It is owned by Emaar Properties. Construction began in 2004 but was not completed until 2009. Non-CG contractors had been commissioned for the task and consequently several faults existed within the structure. Sheikh Wahbi, a senior director with Emaar Properties, was something of a perfectionist and he angrily blasted, 'Why on Earth didn't we get the Cave Girls to make it?' For contractual reasons, it had been necessary to protect the reputation of the original builders, so, under the cover of darkness, a CG named June entirely dismantled the building and flawlessly rebuilt it, with many added improvements. At sunrise, the usually sullen sheikh whooped with joy and exclaimed, 'From the top of this building I can almost touch the moon, June. I'm grateful that you built it so soon. It was poor decision-making from us all to have allowed others to have built something so tall.'

'Touch the moon? It would have been just as easy to have built it all the way up to Neptune, you silly old buffoon!' quipped June. Speaking of June, I once purchased a small cottage at an auction. The property was extremely run-down and uninhabitable. June told me she would look at it for me whilst I picked up some groceries at the supermarket. Upon my return, it was no surprise that I was to find a magnificent, moated castle where the little cottage had been standing just one hour previously.

There are many other examples of CG building constructions, and probably an equally large number, including cities and towns, that have fallen victim to the women's violent destructive traits. Obviously, a CG can destroy a city faster than she can build one. In Italy, the cities of Capua, Herculaneum, Torre, Annunziata and Stabiae were prosperous during the height of the Roman Empire. Two Cave Girls, Abigail and Alice, had been drinking whisky and cola whilst debating the subject of holidays. Abigail enjoyed beach holidays, whilst Alice preferred skiing. As the drinking continued, they became louder and their conversation turned into an argument. For some reason, they decided to end any disagreement by destroying these ancient Roman cities. Still holding their alcoholic beverages, the two ladies smashed and crashed for several seconds. As the huge dust cloud settled enough for the women to see one another, each momentarily giggled before collapsing to the ground in drunken stupor. Sadly, a total of 10,000 people lost their lives during the destruction of these cities. Of course, the doctored official records cite an eruption by Mount Vesuvius. The original name of 'Alcoholics Anonymous' (AA) was 'Abigail Alice' (AA), so named after the intoxicated shenanigans of these CGs.

Speaking of shenanigans, this reminds me that there is a village situated within County Cork in the Republic of Ireland that is called Shanagarry. Twelve thousand years ago, a single property existed on the site where the village lies today. The property was a vast Palladian-style, stately home. It had more than 4,000 rooms. The estate in total covered over 30,000 acres. This was the home of CG Fae, whom I have worked with. She had built her Irish home in just eight minutes and she explained to me that the walls of her palatial residence had looked a trifle too spartan, so she filled the gaps with antlers. Unfortunately, her desire to provide her walls with a more homely feel resulted in the total extinction of *Megaloceros giganteus* (the Irish Elk). Then, deciding the residence now appear cluttered, she angrily pushed the enormous building to the ground and swam to England.

Much later, another CG with the name Hattie, was to have a spare five minutes in which she built the town of Tide Mills in East Sussex, UK. Although the town was flourishing in 1940, the local authority called a meeting to discuss the town's future. At this meeting, Hattie said, 'Well, I can really put this town on the map. I can make some gadgets and show everyone in the town how to make them. They will be known as computer gadgets. They are extremely easy to make and it will not take me long to show you what to do. I can build you a factory in a few seconds if you want. I promise it will be the next big thing; we should call the whole set-up "Microsoft" and our company will easily be worth $1.04 trillion!' However, the local councillors laughed at Hattie.

'She must be mad; I've never heard anything so ridiculous. Microsoft! What a stupid name. It will never make money,' insisted the mayor.

Hattie sighed and wearily said, 'Well, I'm going to leave you little piggies to get on with it and speak to those who are more appreciative of my help.' At this point, she filled her lungs with air. Hattie huffed and she puffed and, with the force of millions of big bad wolves, she then blew the entire settlement down. Several ships in the English Channel were also capsized. The air rushing from her lips carried on, causing major disruption in northern France and was still at hurricane force when it struck Paris!

Essentially, Hattie, for a time, had slipped under the radar, but she is known to have travelled to the USA and during the 1970s and 1980s was in a close friendship with a man named Bill. Today Tide Mills is no more than an eerie collection of wrecked buildings positioned on a bleak landscape. The scene starkly illustrates why one should never laugh at a CG.

The building and engineering skills of CGs enabled them to rapidly construct a series of bridges throughout the world. The longest one was the 'Atlantic Crossing' Suspension Bridge. It spanned almost 6,000 miles. This railway bridge was extremely wide, allowing for twenty lines of track. It enabled non-stop supersonic rail travel, on special trains known as 'Fiesta Ferries', from Notting Hill in London to Rio de Janeiro in Brazil.

Now, although CGs have the intellect and social skills

necessary within 'polite society', they certainly like to party and, when they do, they party hard. I know this better than anyone, especially after seeing them perform in my office at Christmas!

A hundred and thirty thousand years ago, the Atlantic crossing was built, and for over 90,000 years it provided mass transportation for CG revellers as they partied at the carnivals of both cities. Travelling in the trains were highly intoxicated, outright bawdy women. They would regularly humiliate the Neanderthal servants whose role was serving copious quantities of alcohol, repairing damaged carriages and cleaning up CG vomit.

With the party in full swing, the girls would disembark the trains and coolly strut the streets, donning spectacular costumes made from 'dino fuzz' and the feathers from exotic prehistoric birds. The street parties of each carnival would last the entire month of May. Days and nights would be danced away, interspersed with a visit to the vendor selling their preferred street food, jerk velociraptor. Such was the speed of the trains that a CG could easily travel between carnivals as often as she wished. As sleep was prohibited during carnival season, the month of May was when CGs really did party, party, party! The bridge eventually collapsed when the costume of a CG swimming across the Atlantic at 270 m.p.h., became ensnared with a section of the structure.

In 1993, the governments of the UK and France jointly approached CG builders to construct the Channel Tunnel. With Prime Minister John Major's signature secured on the dotted line, his French counterpart President Mitterrand held his pen tantalisingly close above the paperwork. With his pen just about to touch the paper, an aide to Mitterrand interrupted and began whispering about an unrelated matter. This was enough to test the patience of any CG. Unfortunately, the president overheard a CG mutter, 'Oh, for God's sake, just sign it, Napoleon,' and a full-scale diplomatic row ensued. With the French slighted, the deal was off, and the contract was awarded to TransManche Link.

John Major later recited, 'With the atmosphere having become so toxic, I was anxious to ensure the UK's relationship with the Cave Girls should not be adversely affected by some overly-sensitive Frenchman. With this in mind, I commissioned the Cave Girl to erect a wooden shed in the rear garden of 10 Downing Street.'

The small shed was fully completed by a CG in a hundredth of a second, but, at a cost to the taxpayer of fifty billion pounds (the same amount provided to TransManche Link), it remains the most expensive shed of all time. Major justified the CG payment as 'being in the interests of national security'.

Before leaving the subject, it is worth noting that naturally the military implications of CGs are never lost on the security services. As John Deutch, a former director of the Central Intelligence Agency, declared in 1995, 'In the theatre of war, Cave Girls could be our primary asset. They can build faster than the enemy can destroy and they can destroy faster than the enemy can recruit.' He went on say how the United States government must officially deny the existence of CGs, even when challenged with evidence.

CHAPTER SEVEN
CAVE GIRL SPORT

At the MOD in Whitehall is a full-size snooker table which is occasionally used for practice and tournaments for the staff. As part of my research into CG coordination skills and concentration levels, I took possession of this table for a period of two weeks. The CGs had never played snooker before, yet each of the girls on a visit to the table, managed to perform the maximum 147 break, not just once but repeatedly. Even when blindfolded! In 1997, professional snooker player Ronnie O'Sullivan achieved a 147 break against Mick Price at the World Championship. This holds a Guinness world record for the fastest official time of five minutes and twenty seconds. Every CG managed to obtain her 147 break in less than a second. Special cameras were used in the experiment for verification. Even if I moved balls around by hand to create 'impossible snookers', the women were able to play an 'impossible shot' every time and make the pot, again even when blindfolded. Their coordination and spatial awareness are unrivalled.

After testing the twenty available CGs and declaring each 'fully serviceable', I had an in-depth conversation with Nicola and Skylie. They enlightened me to the fact that, throughout CG existence, sport was always popular, and football was played and watched by a great number of CGs. Three hundred thousand years ago, the women had their own version of league football, not that much different in format to the modern English Premier League. Large, magnificent stadiums staged the games in front of capacity crowds. All the players and coaches were CGs and, unsurprisingly, the games were highly physical, high-tempo affairs. The play was very much end-to-end but the footballers showed amazing skill. The matches were extremely exciting and were even dangerous for non-CG spectators, especially for those situated behind the goals. Such was the power of these girl footballers that any goal-bound shot or header would rip through the reinforced netting and cause profound, life-changing injuries or even death to the primitive men who came to watch. At that time there was no health and safety legislation, so death and injury to fans was seen as being 'part of the game'. Cup matches that required penalty shootouts included the added excitement of criminals, vegans and other undesirables being led in chains and placed behind the goals as punishment.

For over five hundred years a club called Jurassic Park Rangers were to dominate the top flight, with an unchanged line up of:

1. Debbie de Gea
2. Gloria Neville
3. Fiona Beckenbauer
4. Pauline Maldini
5. Kylie De Bruyne
6. Joannah Cruyff
7. Doris Maradona
8. Zoe Zidane
9. Lucy Messi
10. Georgina Best

11.Cristine Ronaldo

Petulia Schmeichel and Grace Lineker were the only two substitute players.

Thanks to their remarkable physical strength, combined with supreme physical and mental agility, CGs are perfect athletes. There is not a single sport you could think of that they would not master, even at a first attempt. When one thinks of the Isle of Man, it is reasonable to associate this island with motorcycles and the famous TT Races. However, the creation of the island had a major influence on the girls first throwing rocks, which later became a sport.

Remarkably, an Irish folktale correctly states that the Isle of Man came to exist because of Ireland's legendary hero Fionn mac Cumhaill (commonly known as Finn McCool) being in pursuit of a Scottish giant. As the giant Scot swam back towards Scotland, McCool scooped up a huge mass of rock and clay and hurled it at the escaping giant. McCool overshot and the huge ball of rock and clay fell into the Irish Sea, forming the Isle of Man.

CG Sarmit (from Skylie and the Pussycat Trolls) was witness to the event. Not realising the giant was the intended target, Sarmit scooped up some Irish rock and clay of her own, which she threw, but she used so much power, that her missile travelled right across Britain, over Scandinavia and rocketed across Asia, before finally striking the ground in Arizona, USA. Thus, Sarmit created the Grand Canyon! Finn McCool watched in admiration as Sarmit held a rock-throwing competition with other CGs. The moon was the target. Before this event, the surface of the moon was entirely smooth but, after the Cave Girls had finished their competition, the moon was left as we see it today, severely pitted and cratered.

These women did create and very infrequently use firearms. However, the use of throwing rocks was popular as a sport for hunting birds, as well as large, flying reptiles and big game such as woolly mammoths, rhinoceros and sabre-toothed tigers. Just as, today, some people enjoy a shooting party, these women would organise social gatherings, including 'throwing parties', with animals of any size being the quarry. So, if you are considering 'throwing a party' yourself, you may wish to check the guestlist a second time. Exercise extreme caution with your choice of words as you make the invitations. My advice is to avoid entirely usage of the terms 'throw' and 'throwing' at any type of soiree, and to check the 'small print' on any pet insurance! Fishing was popular with the ladies. Often CGs would swim out to sea and wrestle with giant predatory sea life such as the giant shark, Megalodon, or the ferocious giant whale, Leviathan. Sarmit told me how she was on course to win the Unarmed Pacific Ocean Challenge Competition a few million years ago. Partway through the event, she ripped in half, six megalodons in just four seconds. Unfortunately, she was then disqualified for cheating. When the beautiful, clear-blue waters had turned blood-red, and believing the judges would not notice, she inserted superglue into the blowholes of three leviathans. As punishment, Sarmit received a three-week ban from marine hunting. It was another year before Sarmit was crowned champion.

The noble art of boxing is a passion for these women, although they will never use violence against each other. An average, modern-day, male, heavyweight boxer will deliver a punch of up to around 1700psi. A strike from any CG will be at least 3,400 million psi. However, when required, these superhero women seem to have limitless strength and power. Boxing rings staged many fights in which the women would fight dinosaurs. Usually, the opponent would be a tyrannosaurus, spinosaurus, giganotosaurus or carcharodontosaurus. Initially the contests were over very quickly. After a single punch, the huge and now deceased reptile would be dragged or thrown from the ring. So, to prolong the bouts, the girls would use less power and entertain the crowd, often by dancing around, mocking and jabbing the bewildered opponent. A ring announcer (often referred to as an MC) would introduce the competitors, whip up excitement in the crowd and provide commentary during the fights. These events were extremely popular with CGs and were very 'glitzy'. The Cave Girls in the audience would ditch the usual animal-skin attire and dress up in luxury, formal, evening gowns. The sound of the bell signified the end of each round, and the poor bruised and blooded challenger would stumble and stagger back to its corner, to be 'patched up' by an unpaid, primitive man. Of course, the CG fighter would still be looking sharp and fresh. A little more lipstick, a slight mascara touch-up and she was back, knocking hell out of her hapless opponent until the moment arrived for her to deliver that killer blow!

The standard size ring was seventy-two feet (three times the size of a modern ring). With canvas flooring, ropes and corner pads, it was similar to the boxing rings familiar to us now, except in size. However, ten million years ago in Kenya, CGs fought on the backs of an animal known as Kenyapotamus. This extinct species of hippopotamus was particularly large. Uniquely for an animal of this type, its back was totally flat. The average kenyapotamus carried a level surface area sufficient in size to stage boxing. Consequently, 'hippoback fighting' caught on in a big way in Kenya. To many, watching combat sport on a moving 'platform' offered greater appeal. In search for added variety on the entertainment front, other species of creatures were captured, the highly trainable *Gigantopithecus blacki* being one of them. It stood three metres high and weighed over 500kg, making it the largest ape to have ever lived. Its size and strength had ensured its safety from predators and its population was at an extremely healthy level, until that is, CGs introduced it to the world of boxing. The apes were happy to be dressed in gloves and shorts, and they certainly enjoyed their shadow boxing, ten kilometre runs, skipping with skipping ropes and gym sessions. Their CG trainers taught them the essential skills needed to be fearless and confident fighters. The hairy giants, who were probably the inspiration for the fictional King Kong, became super fit and experts in self-defence. They were quick to learn and had been equipped with a level of coaching second to none. The modern and recognised boxing positions of upright stance, semi crouch and full crouch became second nature to these giant-fisted beasts, who were more than a match for most mortal beings. Meanwhile, Nicola was at the height of her sporting popularity 300,000 years ago. She was undefeated (as were all CGs) in all bouts against dinosaurs, polar bears, cave bears and megatheriums (giant sloths). How would she fare against these powerful monsters that had been specifically trained for boxing by other CGs?

Large numbers of well-dressed women watched ringside, whilst many more watched the live, televised broadcasts of Nicola slaughtering ape challenger after ape challenger. Nicola had displayed great self-control to make the contests last sufficient time to make for 'good television'. Nicola's restraint was, however, temporary and her demeanour changed: she began to display all the classic characteristics of behaviour that my psychological therapist would describe as 'frenzy mode'. Whilst in this state, none of the apes was able to stay alive for more than a fraction of a second. Each one would have been punched over two hundred and fifty times and any of those punches would have resulted in death! Organisers vainly attempted to prolong viewing time by introducing multiple giant apes into the ring simultaneously, but all this did, was fuel Nicola's frenzy. Weeks earlier, the *Gigantopithecus blacki* population stood at six million. However, as boxing had grown phenomenally popular with CGs, live *Gigantopithecus blacki*s were to become only available online, but by then it was too late. The animals continued 'selling like hot cakes' as the girls used them as punch bags. By the end of a single weekend worldwide event, dubbed 'the Blockbuster Boxing Bonanza', not one of these magnificent apes remained alive. They were gone forever. I asked Nicola to sum the event up in her own words. She said, 'I had the best time. It was awesome!'

CHAPTER EIGHT
WORKING GIRLS

The topics concerned within these texts are clearly most sensitive and I have only been able to provide yourself the scantest of detail for reasons concerning my own personal security. My revelations are released under the most unreasonable and dire circumstances imaginable, nervously writing away in total darkness, fearful that at any moment a government assassin will silently enter the room and fire a bullet in the back of my skull! Yet, you deserve to know the extent of the lies and deceit that countless generations around the world have been subjected to by numerous international governments. I can only pray that this message reaches you.

In truth, it is not known exactly how many CGs exist within the world, but it is certain, that they are at large within modern society, hopefully using their superhuman talents for good. My research suggests this is often the case. I have accessed police files going back decades, which provide conclusive proof of their many interventions. Armed and ruthless drug dealers have been apprehended, burglars and muggers being thrown hundreds of feet into the air and the corpses of carjackers propelled distances of ten miles. There is even the fascinating example of an especially violent and loathsome loan shark who was heavily involved in blackmail and people smuggling. CCTV images show him in conversation with a woman wearing leopard-skin clothing who clearly kicks this horrible man into the air. He vanishes from view but my colleagues at NASA, confirmed his body travelled though outer space and beyond our solar system!

I worked with all the Cave Girls on the UK government payroll. This was, by far, the most interesting assignment I have been tasked with. Yet it was equally frustrating. They knew I was studying them and each of the women had an intellect so advanced, I considered my task impossible. Expecting a human to merely understand a CG is equivalent of expecting a hot water bottle to not only understand Professor Stephen Hawking as a person but also absorb all the knowledge he acquired during his lifetime!

These women laughed at me when I demanded their respect. They laughed at me when I sought their cooperation. They laughed at me when I sipped orange juice from a glass. The only time they did not laugh was when I told them a joke. By and large, they humiliated me. My only comfort was that I was not alone in experiencing this. Skylie was almost in stitches when in 2009, Usain Bolt set the fastest one hundred metres with his 9.58 seconds. 'I could have done three laps round the world in that time!' she quipped.

Then in 1997 'dizzy blonde' Cimberley sat opposite world champion chess player Anatoly Karpov. The Russian angrily resigned in just one move. Although Cimberley poked fun at him and directed highly offensive and personal remarks at him, Karpov begged her to give him chess lessons before he next played an opponent. Several years later, during a television interview, Karpov revealed he had 'learned more about the tactics of chess in one minute from that blonde thing than from anyone else'. Until she had met the Russian, Cimberley had never even seen a chessboard.

I hoped CGs working under the umbrella of the MOD would not become institutionalised (although there was no reason to think they would be). I was also curious as to how under 'loose and minimal supervision' they would cope in the working world, amongst the civilian population and wearing non-CG clothing. I started the experiment with Nicola, who qualified as a nurse and was very rapidly promoted to senior staff nurse. I went to visit her when she was on shift in the Accident and Emergency Department. She looked so smart in her uniform, and it appeared obvious that she was highly competent, efficient and professional.

'Hi, Nicola. How are things with you?' I asked.

'I just love being a nurse,' she replied, her face beaming with pride. 'Every day I look forward to getting to work and caring for the patients.'

With a radio tuned to the local station, pop music quietly played. The scene was peaceful and I was pleased that things were going well, not just for Nicola but also for her colleagues and the public. At exactly four p.m. the music stopped, and the newscaster announced that a large escaped bull was roaming around the Seftmore area of the town, with the police asserting the animal being dangerous and not to be approached.

Nicola gave me a knowing look, immediately removed a scalpel from a drawer and began to laugh. 'Nursing is okay when there is nothing more exciting to do. Time for action. Fancy a beef burger tonight, Crawford?'

I was never going to be able to stop her. The next morning, the front page of the *Seftmore Observer* carried the headline 'Hero Nurse Saves Children from Maniac Bull'. Possibly because of her 'occupation', the newspaper had played down the fact that Nicola had killed the bull by breaking its neck with her bare hands and, using a surgical scalpel, butchered the animal in the street. Its editor had chosen to emphasise that the finest cuts of meat were fed to the homeless. Before moving on to Skylie, I considered the feasibility of just asking Nicola not to listen to radio news bulletins in future. On second thoughts, Nicola is just too great a risk to remain at large.

I arrived at the luxury apartment the MOD had recently provided to Skylie. She made me a coffee and told me she was happy with her accommodation. We chatted for a while about her plans on becoming a high school teacher and how quickly this could be achieved. She pressed the TV remote control. There was Jeremy Paxman, hosting *University Challenge*.

As Skylie turned her attention to the television, a spotty eighteen-year-old, ginger-haired lad incorrectly answered 'Hallstatt' to the question 'Which village near Vienna is the site of the hunting lodge where the Habsburg Crown Prince Rudolf and his paramour Mary Vetsera committed suicide in mysterious circumstances in 1889?'

'Hallstatt!' exclaimed Skylie. 'How thick is he? The answer is Mayerling.' She then chuckled.

As Paxman rattled off the questions like a machine gun, Skylie 'returned rapid fire' with a hundred per cent of correct answers. But when she started supplying correct answers to his part questions: 'Which—', 'What name—', 'In cytogenetics—', 'Often featuring—', 'At—', 'W—', I switched the television off and joked, 'That will do, Skylie;

no need to be a smarty pants.' I continued, 'Seriously, though, I think you would be a great teacher.'

'I hope so. I like kids and I could teach them any subject.'

Then something happened that made me realise I must return this CG back to base immediately. She was becoming irritated with a neighbour, who was now slamming doors and she was eager for me to leave. When she started humming the tune 'Spinning Around', I said, 'Get your stuff, young lady, I can't leave you here. I know what you are thinking about doing when I go.' It was not long before I returned Skylie to Whitehall. However, during the drive back to base, she taught me that Queen Boudicca had not, in fact died, in AD 61. She is still very much alive and kicking. After slaying 7,000 Romans and their British supporters, she set up roots in Australia. Skylie was just as willing to impart that Maid Marian was in fact a CG. Robin Hood had been little more than a fantasist, inspired by Maid Marian's frequent bouts of extreme violence that she had directed at wealthy people. Little John, Friar Tuck, Will Scarlet and Alan-a-Dale were not 'merry men', as portrayed. They all lived very much in fear of CG Marian. There is also doubt as to whether 'Much' really was 'the miller's son'! An uneasy peace was finally established during the 1500s between the Sheriff of Nottingham and Maid Marian. With his own men having been 'wiped', the Sheriff paid Maid Marian protection money in exchange for not robbing from the rich and giving to the poor.

Sarmit initially found success within the motor trade. Too much success, actually! When I visited 'SAS' (Sarmit's Automotive Services) in Hampshire, I could not help but be impressed. CG Sarmit had, by hand, demolished the old, ramshackle building units that had previously formed Norcliffe Industrial Park. The former tenants and the site proprietor had all mysteriously disappeared. However, the government ensured that everyone in Hampshire would be so involved in the search for — this time — a black-and-white cat called Humphrey, that such trivial matters such as missing people would not be newsworthy!

With gleaming new and aesthetically pleasing buildings, brushed with that certain 'Cave Girl touch', the whole area resembled a Utopian health spa village, certainly not a dated and grimy industrial centre. She was carrying out servicing and repairs to cars, motorcycles, vans, lorries, coaches and buses. Sarmit was buying and selling cars too. In no time at all, this CG would transform an old rusty and wrecked Ford Fiesta into a Bugatti La Voiture Noire, and selling it for over ten million pounds sterling. I asked her what she intended to do with a tatty Fiat Punto that was looking incredibly sad in the corner of a workshop. Before I could blink, in its place was a fine example of a Porsche 911. Sarmit sold all makes and models, as many as twenty a day. Incredibly, she could repair countless motor vehicles, each better than new.

Such was Sarmit's engineering skill and her own physical strength, that much of the mechanical equipment housed within her state-of-the-art workshops remained redundant and she required no additional staff. She operated a vehicle recovery service for all types of vehicle. Unfortunately, this was to receive unwelcome attention from the police. Since the SAS had been in operation, speed cameras had detected a significant increase in the number of speeding lorries and other large vehicles.

As these cases were investigated, Sarmit could clearly be seen towing enormous articulated juggernauts, complete with fully loaded trailers, at speeds exceeding one hundred m.p.h. Even more remarkable was that the CG was not at the wheel of any recovery vehicle. She was pulling the broken-down lorries herself with just a chain around her waist. She was even smiling for the camera! Under pressure from the Ministry of Defence, the police had little difficulty in sweeping Sarmit's road traffic offences 'under the carpet'; however, when Sarmit began crushing the vehicles of late-paying customers, her enterprise had to cease, especially as people had become traumatised at witnessing 'a young woman squashing cars into cubes with her bare hands'.

In 2020, there is only one nuclear power plant on the African continent. Located approximately twenty-three kilometres north of Cape Town, stands the two-reactor Koeberg nuclear power station. There have been several occasions over the years where technical problems have resulted in a loss of power from the station, but it happened particularly often, towards the end of 2005. During these episodes, most of the Western Cape has been left without power. Then on 18th and 19th February 2007 this part of South Africa was again subject to power cuts, after a controlled shutdown was required.

The government of South Africa was determined to ensure that the 6.6 million inhabitants and the industrial centre of Cape Town would not be starved of electricity any further but the technical problems at Koeberg were so extraordinarily complex, that scientists were baffled. There were grave safety and economic concerns so there could be no delay. Swift and decisive action was required so, secretly, the South African government enlisted the help of my CG Katy. A flight was booked for me and Katy, but the CG told me she would get there quicker if she swam and, sure enough, she was already in the Koeberg power station staff gym when I arrived. The treadmill and cycle machines that she was working out on had been adapted, by Katy herself, to generate more than enough electricity for the region's needs. During her exercising, she cast an eye over the plans and technical drawings of the power station and called out a number of instructions. Within minutes, the atomic plant was now back to full and safe working order. Katy made some modifications. She wrote a list of 'tips' for the technicians to follow should there be future problems. Typically, years later when the list was needed, it could not be found because the cleaner had thrown it away. However, that was not Katy's fault!

Whilst in South Africa, Katy and I decided a spot of sightseeing was in order and so visited Rorke's Drift, Natal Province; site of the famous 1879 Battle of Rorke's Drift. We even met some authentic Zulu warriors and I was puzzled at why they surveyed Katy so nervously. She was wearing trainers, denim shorts and a T-shirt. One of them said anxiously, 'Cave Girl'! The group of about ten warriors, who had been absolutely fine with me, backed away from her and then began running very fast over the dusty hills, as if their lives depended upon it, until they were out of sight.

'What was all that about?' I asked.

'I have absolutely no idea,' she replied petulantly.

The owners of the power station were so grateful that they arranged for our return to the UK by luxury cruise ship. During the crossing, Katy told me how she loved the sea. What I did not expect to learn from her was that HMS *Bounty* was a small vessel; I thought it had been a large ship. It had been purchased by the Royal Navy, having formerly been a merchant ship. The captain, William Bligh, and his crew had been on route on the *Bounty*, officially to transport breadfruit plants from Pacific Ocean islands to the West Indies. It is well-documented that the mission was not fulfilled because Acting Lieutenant Fletcher Christian instigated a mutiny. Popular fiction, emanating from government cover-ups, portray William Bligh as a tyrant, a bully whose behaviour was always likely to result in a mutiny amongst his crew. It was convenient for the UK government and the Royal Navy to depict this image of him. According to Katy, Bligh was a 'decent and fair captain, at all times deeply concerned for the well-being and happiness of his men'. Unfortunately, Fletcher Christian had spotted a CG swimming alongside the *Bounty* in open water. Upon looking up, she recognised him as having been the man who stole her glass of beer from a tavern along the River Thames in London two months previously. She angrily shouted, 'When you reach the West Indies, I will be waiting, and you will regret stealing my beer, Fletch!'

The naval officer witnessed her strength and power as she swam on ahead at such speed; the wake almost capsized the vessel. Christian was so terrified and, without telling anybody his reasons, managed to persuade others to mutiny, but only so that he could avoid getting his 'just deserts', in accordance with Cave Girl justice! Katy and I continued with the cruise and I was fascinated watching her in the casino. This CG had not previously stepped foot in one before, yet within about four hours she had amassed a fortune equal to the national net worth of a European country. Despite being banned from entering the casino in future, it was too late to save the previously large and successful cruise company, which went into liquidation owing Katy trillions of pounds! Back in London, I checked with the Ministry of Defence archive records, which confirmed not only that had Captain Bligh sailed through 'Cave Girl infested waters' on 28th April 1789 but also that Lieutenants John Chard and Gonville Bromhead of the Royal Engineers, had managed to acquire the assistance of a CG during the Battle of Rorke's Drift.

I knew that it is possible for CGs to co-exist harmoniously with the public because they do, but in the interests of global security, believe it essential to identify as many scenarios as possible that would trigger CG aggression in everyday life. As far as governments are concerned, there is clearly a delicate balance in being able to identify CGs, so as to recruit them, keeping their existence a secret, and obviously preventing CGs' uncontrollable aggression in avoiding human extinction.

With the above in mind, I decided to travel by bus with Catherine (the Great) to Hampton Court Palace in East Molesey, a twenty-minute journey. We waited at the bus stop. I kept a discreet distance from Catherine, to monitor her independent behaviour. All was fine at first, with the CG waiting patiently for the bus. With the digital display above the bus shelter indicating that our bus was due to arrive in five minutes, I was hopeful for an incident-free excursion, but then a car parked at the bus stop with the driver chatting on his mobile phone. Catherine turned to me with a look of disapproval. 'That's not right. He should not park here. It's a bus stop. Well, if he thinks he's a bus, he's taking me to Hampton Court!' she yelled.

Before I could stop her, the CG had flung open the front passenger door and plonked herself next to the shocked driver. There were a few angry verbal exchanges between the two in the car before Catherine snatched the driver's mobile, crushed it in her hand and threw the remains into his face. The angry woman exited the vehicle and lifted its entire front with her fingers under the wheel arch and flung the offending car with such force that it flattened a 'Keep Left' bollard thirty metres away, before travelling the same distance again and only coming to rest upon smashing though a glass-fronted fish and chip shop.

Luckily the bus arrived, now with room to pull in, and the only other person to have witnessed the incident was an extremely elderly, male Zimmer frame user, who was laughing hysterically with seeming approval at what he had just seen. With the audible alarms from the car and shop now sounding, Catherine assisted this gentleman onto the bus. Now we were all aboard, we began the journey and all was well again!

The former world leader began looking around the bus. She smiled at a young mother cradling a baby. The baby was fidgety and crying; mum was becoming stressed and embarrassed as she vainly attempted to quieten her increasingly irritable infant. At this point, a woman in her late sixties, seated a few rows back, tutted and called out to the mother, 'Excuse me, dear, please stop your baby crying.

It's so awfully annoying. I can hardly hear myself think!'

Well, that was it. Like a shot, Catherine removed the child from the mother and plonked it into the arms of the woman who 'could not hear herself think'. Her long, black but heavily greying locks of hair stood on end as the CG bellowed, 'There you go. See how good you are, Mary Fucking Poppins!'

I left my seat and returned the now-screaming child to mum and ushered Catherine to the seat next to me. I just did not know what to say to her. Catherine turned her head and must have shot the intolerant sourpuss such a look, that she immediately requested the driver to let her off the bus premature of reaching a recognised bus stop. My CG then smiled lovingly at the young mother and child until we reached the end of the journey.

The bus pulled up outside the palace gates and briefly we sat together on a bench within the grounds. 'How do you think it went?' she asked.

'You know full well how it went, Catherine. The incident with the car: you know we are trying to keep things a secret. I expect the town centre CCTV supervisor will be rewarded with a knighthood for keeping his gob shut, but we shouldn't be giving out knighthoods willy-nilly, to everyone who keeps stum about you Cave Girls. I'm the one that has to report back to the prime minister. I don't like any unnecessary paperwork, but I do enjoy jaunts out in this country and other, more exotic locations, so I don't want them to cut our budget!'

The ex-empress of Russia began writing on several pieces of white paper with a ballpoint pen she had removed from her handbag. I was mesmerised at the speed of her writing, as within approximately five seconds, each double side of the writing paper was entirely filled with her immaculate handwriting. I watched her as she picked up a tennis ball-sized stone from a flower bed, and she wrapped the writing paper around it. Finally, she secured the paper to the stone with a large elastic band. With a distinct swooshing sound, Catherine threw the object across the sky in a westerly direction. She then sat next to me, yet almost immediately jumped back up to produce a most majestic, one-handed catch of an object travelling east. It was a stone wrapped in blue writing paper.

'What is going on?' I asked.

'Hattie, you know, had a thing with Bill Gates in America. She's still out there and we are penfriends. We like to write to each other. We are quite old-fashioned about that,' she replied, smiling as she read Hattie's letter. 'Come on. Let's go and see the maze.'

Catherine led our way through the 'Wilderness Gardens'. At the entrance to the maze, she stopped, and I noticed a change in her mood. Her lips had become thinner and I believed she was now angry.

'This is the labyrinth. You have put the minotaur in there!' she growled.

'No, of course not. This is not Greece and the minotaur was killed by Theseus,' I said, frantically thinking what I could say next to prevent inevitable carnage.

The CG replied, 'Well, it was actually killed by Georgina, but I'm not taking any chances of there being other minotaurs. I always wanted to destroy one of them!'

Quick as a flash, she was gone. Before I had time to enter, people, dogs and picnic hampers were being tossed over the high hedges and out of the maze. I had managed to get one foot through the entrance when I met Catherine on her return from the centre of the three-hundred-year-old maze.

'Just kidding with you, Crawford. I knew the minotaur wasn't in there; I just wanted to see what you would do. It was so worth it just to see your face.' Catherine bent forward, almost crying with laughter. I saw at least twenty visitors prostrate on the grass outside the maze. Some were moving and groaning, others still and silent. Dogs were whimpering as they stood, staring down at their fallen owners. On hearing the two-tone sirens of emergency vehicles nearing the royal estate, I was anxious to leave. Catherine, however, was in no rush; she remained looking and laughing at the feeble and stricken day trippers. Each one had been provided with an unforgettable experience!

After much pleading from me, Catherine reluctantly agreed to leave, and, not willing to risk public transport a second time, I arranged for a MOD car to transport us back to Whitehall. With Catherine now in her quarters and watching *Coronation Street* on her television, I left the building, but not before I heard a loud, male voice call out, 'Crawford. The Met Police Commissioner is not happy, and the PM wants a full report by eight a.m. tomorrow morning.' I closed my eyes, sighed and left the building for fresh air and to clear my head.

It was such a relief when I learned later that the victims of the Hampton Court maze 'rampage' had not suffered injuries more severe than moderate concussion. Catherine had been truthful when she told me she was 'just kidding'. At the palace, she had programmed herself to 'stun mode' to avoid fatalities, but I was angry that she had prolonged my stress by not informing me of this herself.

One lady I would have preferred to have spent more time in 'stun mode' was CG Natalie. Under the pretext of my 'research assistant', Nat once accompanied me to the Department of Infectious Diseases, at Imperial College London, following its request to the MOD for my expertise. Natalie donned a laboratory gown over civilian clothing. Despite having perfect Cave Girl vision, Natalie wore spectacles to portray a more 'plausible character to an intellectual audience.'

Whilst at this great institution, my CG 'assistant' was invaluable, and within an hour, had formulated a cure for all allergic diseases, arthritis, the common cold and psoriasis. As a reward, the principal of the Department of Bioengineering led us to a room and showed us a collection of large and extremely rare spiders, whose venom was of scientific interest. In financial terms, they were all so high in value that it was not possible to have them insured. He removed from a glass tank a huge, hairy, orange, eight-legged monster and placed it in a smaller, open-topped transparent container. Addressing Nat, the scientist enthusiastically said, 'Look, darling, I'm overcome with excitement every time I see this bad boy. His name is John. He's the only one left in the world and has been for many years. Do you know what he is?'

'Obviously, it's a Bohemiam stobe spider,' replied the CG.

The principal nodded and the expression on his face portrayed delighted surprise that she answered correctly. Repeating the process with another equally large and revolting creature, he said, 'The deadliest spider on the planet. Twice the size of a goliath birdeater, its venom is so lethal that a single bite will kill an adult elephant within five minutes. The fangs will literally pierce armour. He is an evolutionary miracle. However, in the natural world, he serves no purpose other than controlling the numbers of giant mango lizards, which would otherwise dominate the tropical southern hemisphere. I regard him as a pet and I love him. His name is Rupert. Rupert will prove a great investment towards my retirement. You see, young lady, the prize specimen you see before you will again compete in the World Spider Show, judged annually in Los Angeles. Rupert has been champion three years running, and he carries a stud value of an incredible 300,000 US dollars, making him the world's most valuable invertebrate and will live and remain fertile for the next seventy years. He has a lovely temperament. I consider him a true friend. Do you know what he is?'

'Rupert is quite clearly a Panama manese zebra spider,' said Nat.

As the principal went up to more glass tanks containing his huge eight-legged friends, he said, 'Well done! Go to the top of the class! These are other spiders that I am very fond of…'

He was interrupted from finishing his sentence by the sound of glass breaking on the floor. As he turned, his eyes descended on Natalie's size six shoe being placed on Rupert's head and body. With its frantically moving legs pointed upwards, she twisted her foot and its legs dropped to the floor and became motionless.

'No! Stop!' he shouted. However, John was to

immediately suffer the same fate. Natalie then began smashing the glass homes of the other arachnids. She grabbed all the remaining nine with her hands before each was squashed and gunk oozed from between her fingers.

'Just going to wash my hands,' she said, as she left the room.

'She is mad. She's killed Rupert and all the spiders,' he quietly said, as he sobbed into his handkerchief. With my feet involuntarily sliding on the now-slippery floor, I also left the room, collected CG Nat and exited the building, minus the customary handshakes or 'goodbyes' for the hosts. Perhaps I should have been scornful of Natalie's actions, but the pair of us burst out laughing. Actually, the spider episode tickled me for the rest of the day.

Despite the Imperial College fiasco, I believed Nat could exist and function almost unnoticed by the public, unless she brought attention on herself. The temporary accommodation issued to her was a spacious, detached, four-bedroomed family home in Godalming, Surrey. The rear garden was fully enclosed, measuring one square acre, with a large lawn. She had a set of golf clubs with her and was practising her swing as I approached. She then put a ball on the tee, struck it with a driver and the ball vanished from sight.

'I think you overhit that one a bit, Natalie,' I commented smugly.

'No, I haven't; it has just dropped down the eighth hole at Royal Melbourne in Australia. That is where I am practising. So far today, every shot has been a hole-in-one. Stick that in your pipe and smoke it, Crawford!' I was not going to debate the point any further, as she was certainly being truthful.

'Just thought I would pop over to see how you were getting on with your venture into the world of business. I do not recall what it was you were doing,' I said.

'Momentously fantastic. You should be so proud of me, Crawford. I have such great business acumen!' she said, as she put away the golf club and lit a cigarette. Well, how could it have slipped my mind? Nat had created a pest control business. Concerningly (as my department was trying to keep CGs' existence confidential) she had named it 'Cave Girl Pest Controllers'. She had formed a partnership with Canadian CG, Christine. The Canadian wing of the operation was named 'Christine's Critter Crushing Company'.

The two girls masterminded a slick and sophisticated worldwide operation enabling them to be contacted by anyone in any country in need of vermin eradication. Rodents, birds and insects initially formed the bulk of the work. Eventually these women were hired by local authorities, as well as individuals, for the extermination of foxes and badgers. They even culled alligators, crocodiles and wild boar. Although their promotional literature boasted that no firearms, poisons or chemicals were used, knowing how sadistic CGs can be, firearms, poisons and chemicals would likely have been preferred by the vermin! Still, hiring a CG exterminator is the most effective way of eradicating the unwanted. That is guaranteed.

Stubbing out her cigarette on the head of a large shiny black beetle, she giggled and said, 'I'm really into my work and it is so necessary. Come indoors, Crawford. I will show you my office.'

I browsed the large list of orders. She had been busy indeed. Glancing at the settled invoices, I noticed, her services were not cheap, but it was apparent she was a prompt and reliable solution. In a single day she had killed: eight alligators in Alabama, two crocodiles in Botswana, a rogue elephant in Goa, two hundred ant nests in France, a seagull in Crystal Palace and, for some reason, a canary in Ipswich.

It was astonishing, the high volume of her clientele who were male. Firefighters, police officers, soldiers, judges, lumberjacks, builders, bailiffs, professional rugby players and nightclub doormen from every continent were on her list. Equally amazing were the nature of their orders. For example, a lumberjack from British Columbia placed an order for the destruction of one bee in the cab of his truck. This was far from being an isolated case. Also, many men had emailed their gratitude:

'Thank you so much, Natalie. I don't know what I would have done without you. That moth was so scary!' (Igor, powerlifter, Moscow)

'You're my hero, Natalie. I was hiding in the corner of my bedroom for hours until I called you. Thanks for turning up so quick and stamping on the spider. I had been petrified!' (Luther, doorman, London)

'I know you wrote off my Mercedes Sprinter van squashing that greenfly but I would recommend you to anyone. Thanks again, Cave Girl Pest Controllers.' (Bob, construction worker, Manchester)

'Amazing service once again! One minute after calling Cave Girl Pest Controllers, the job was done. The rats were dead. Natalie even cleaned up most of the guts which had splattered all over my floors, ceilings, doors, windows and walls of my shop.' (Darren, master butcher, Frankfurt)

'I cannot thank you enough, Natalie. Cockroaches have blighted my business for years. Then I called you, so no more cockroaches. You were so discreet that the customers hardly noticed. Come back any time for a meal on the house!' (Ammon, restaurateur, Cairo)

I examined more of Nat's paperwork and clearly the partnership was working well. Projections were forecasting the business concern would, within days, eclipse the turnover of their largest rivals and had plans of rebranding to simply 'Cave Girl Crushers'. However, in a filing cabinet drawer labelled 'cretins', I read a letter from a Mr Bjorn Larsen, from Norway.

Whilst Mr Larsen expressed gratitude that the moose that had previously been eating his ornamental shrubs had been dispatched, he was far from satisfied that, initially, Natalie had mistaken his wife as being the moose and mounted her head on the living room wall before he came home from work. The accompanying photograph of the late Mrs Larsen does explain how the confusion in identity arose, but I told Natalie the situation was unacceptable and she must cease trading with immediate effect. With the Canadian Security Intelligence Service alerted, Christine was questioned by agents in Ottawa before being sent to London, where she became a highly prized member of my CG 'family'.

The uncertain results of CGs performing pest control operations for the public led to my decision that they only be deployed on this type of activity, under the directive of selected national security services. With Christine eager to prove her worth, she landed her first official assignment in April 2000. An American agent, having been posted to a mission, had been based within a Berlin hotel. It was standard CIA procedure for the agents to electronically record their own voices and provide a running commentary whilst on operations. The following is a transcript from Agent O'Brien:

'I am Agent Simon O'Brien, based in Europe and engaged within location Alpha One Seven. Current assignment: investigation into the unexplained brutal mutilations of ten CIA agents in as many weeks. Only one of them lived long enough to utter the words "it had eight legs. It had eight legs" before taking his last breath. Well, I'll get to the bottom of this. I must. I owe it to those great guys.'

There is the sound of O'Brien entering a bathroom and urinating into the toilet bowl whilst humming the tune of 'The Star-Spangled Banner'.

'There is a spider in the bath! God damn it... The culprit has found me. I knew Saddam Hussein's scientists had been working on the creation of genetically engineered killer spiders to penetrate Europe. Well. Looks like they did it. All my twenty years as a Navy Seal could not have prepared me for what I am now looking at.'

O'Brien leaves the room and telephones the Pentagon.

'I confirm, O'Brien. Alpha One Seven. I will need fifty heavily armed marines, a bazooka, at least five choppers for air support and two tanks. Better have a nuclear warhead primed on standby. This is serious shit going on in Europe!'

There is a minute pause whilst he is instructed by the Pentagon by phone. Then he continues slowly and quizzically.

'You're calling a Cave Girl?' Almost immediately Christine arrives, to be greeted with O'Brien's snarling of, 'With all due respect, young lady, you're going to need protective clothing and backup!'

In her typical bright and breezy manner, Christine can be heard on the voice recording to say, 'Move out of my way. It's probably still in the bath. Follow me.'

Agent O'Brien became so distressed, at the utter horror of what he witnessed, that he took early retirement and, out of respect for him and his family, I have decided to edit from this transcript the remainder of his words and crying. However, the most brutal act imaginable was to take place... the CG lifted her foot into the bath, placing it directly onto what was no more than a common house spider!

In 2003, Christine again volunteered her services; promising a swift and decisive end to the Iraq War. Prime Minister Tony Blair welcomed the suggestion. However, US president George W. Bush had been present during a NATO training exercise in Alaska that Christine had been part of. This is probably the reason he vetoed the move and I clearly remember his words: 'Using Christine to stop a war would be like using a sledgehammer to crack a walnut. She would obliterate the entire Middle East! I don't know what has got into Tony's head. And they say I'm a warmonger!'

Working on her own, as an independent lady builder, was Tracey. A true CG, her work is worthy of the highest accolade. Flawless constructions were created in minutes, even those several storeys high. She, of course, would assemble any flat-pack furniture in a millisecond or build the grandest of mansions before you could say 'Bob's your uncle'. Tracey also had a good business head and owned a flourishing building company. All her work was handmade with no tools or machinery. As her favourite jobs were renovation projects, she named her firm 'Tracey's Transformations'. The title served her well in attracting her preferred orders. The consequences of disputing Tracey's invoices, or not settling punctually, were most dire. Not only would she destroy her masterpiece buildings (even with people inside at the time); she would also target friends and family members too! So, when Prince Andrew quibbled over the price of a patio, she installed for him, whilst he was visiting his friend Jeffrey Epstein, I had to step in fast!

'Tracey, do you remember that time in the twelfth century when you kicked a ball against that tower in Pisa?' I asked.

'Yes, of course I do,' she confirmed. 'I grabbed hold of it to stop it falling down. I secured it, so I could walk away, but they should have built it properly in the first place. I only tapped the ball really; it couldn't have been travelling at more than 4,000 m.p.h.'

'Well, as you are so good at stopping things falling down, I would like you to travel to lots of countries where there's going to be an earthquake. Your job will be to stop the biggest or most important buildings from falling. How does that sound?'

'Sounds like fun, Crawford!' replied Tracey.

'Good girl, Tracey. I will keep you posted,' I said, hoping my offer would distract her from the other business that was on her mind concerning the Duke of York! One month later came the most powerful earthquake ever to strike San Francisco. With Tracey already in position, the residents slept soundly and undisturbed in their beds. Not a single building was damaged.

GCHQ, or the Government Communications Headquarters, based in Cheltenham, has now existed for over one hundred years and is now also the parent organisation of the National Cyber Security Centre (NCSC). GCHQ undertakes the most sensitive of tasks in keeping the UK safe. During World War Two, it was instrumental in breaking German codes and today operates the most sophisticated equipment necessary in monitoring worldwide telephone calls, emails, voicemails etc. of individuals and organisations perceived as potential threats to UK security. Their work attracts considerable suspicion, with allegations regarding misuse of data collected, as well as some conspiracy theorists commentating that the existence of the organisation is clear evidence that we are all under close and constant surveillance in a 'Big Brother' society. Certainly, GCHQ is an eavesdropping centre with a particularly long reach.

I performed several trials with Cave Girls associated with their eavesdropping and surveillance skills. I had prior knowledge of their sense of hearing, specially adapted for hunting purposes. A CG in England can hear a flea hopping in New Zealand and would even be able to pinpoint the exact whereabouts of that flea from just one hop. What I did discover, was that CGs have even mastered the art of teleportation, which is unfortunate for the Kiwi flea. Teleportation renders all other forms of transportation unnecessary, yet is seldom used as the girls consider it 'the height of laziness'. The luxury motor cars that they drove millions of years ago were merely fashion accessories and other modes of transport such as train travel, as with the

Fiesta Ferries, were utilised to 'enhance the experience of the journey'.

One trial involved a total shutdown of GCHQ for three months, with one girl monitoring all verbal and digital communications occurring at the time. She was able to record the vast amount of material collected on an electronic device of her own design and making (no equivalent piece of equipment existed). Her device was, in fact, no more than an electronic notepad with a memory large enough to store an infinite amount of information. As she listened with nothing more than her ears, she would, at incredible speed, jot down every piece of human communication happening at that time across the entire planet and in space.

The world during the period of this trial was the most stable it had been for decades. As the CG could hear everything, she was in the best position to direct all operations, and, as a result, all terrorist and organised criminal activities were disrupted. GCHQ was redundant and the commercial opportunities, i.e., selling Cave Girl 'tip-offs' to foreign governments, were identified. However, there was a conflict of interest involving UK politicians. As a CG was able to hear everything, she would be able to hear and record the private conversations of the political elite. Every intimate detail. As so many public figures are less than lily-white, a secret internal cabinet vote was held and the politicians within the UK government chose to place their reputations ahead of our national security. GCHQ was reopened and the CG was asked to close her ears. During its existence, *The News of the World* shamelessly asked me to sell stories emanating from CG eavesdropping.

Whilst working for the MOD, I not only recruited other CGs from around the world; the women themselves assisted me in producing shiny, spanking, brand-new Cave Girls. Thanks to my effort, the UK boasts an impressive arsenal of these women. As previously mentioned, CGs do not officially exist, yet, although there is no written reference to them within the Geneva Convention, their use is all but outlawed by it. That said, the British armed forces have several within its ranks. In fact, in the days when soldiers could be executed by firing squad, occasionally the squad was replaced by a CG, who would perform the execution to save ammunition. Records were falsified to conceal the cause of death. The German Shepherd dog is a favourite canine breed for police forces around the world. It was only when female dog handler Mia replaced her police-issued dog with a pack of ten grey wolves, that some became suspicious of her. During the early 1960s, the officer was a familiar, if unwelcome, sight on the streets of Munich.

Traditional vetting procedures adopted by the armed forces and police are unreliable in identifying CGs during the recruitment process. Consequently, as the confrontational element of such work holds appeal to the girls, some CGs have entered the services and remained undetected for years until a 'trigger situation' occurs. (The T. Rex tribute concert caused a trigger situation, because the of the dinosaur association with the name.) For this reason, I sought a means of safely simulating trigger situations early in their careers. In this way, their senior officers would know exactly who the CGs were. They would record the details of those women and either sparingly utilise their extraordinary talents themselves or would transfer them to my department. A CG audit is carried out annually.

During even a mild trigger situation, the woman will display violence on such a scale that humans must remain a minimum of three hundred miles away for at least eight hours. Any living creature in sight faces certain death. Some women remain deceptively easy-going whilst in 'trigger syndrome', whilst others will fly into an uncontrollable rage. In either case, the woman is equally destructive and deadly. My preferred locations were the North and South Poles. Not only are they remote; the cold air tends to calm their tempers more quickly than in warmer climates. At the South Pole, there is a permanent CG research facility that is shared by NATO members. At the chosen site, I would leave a selection of flashcards, each displaying a different picture. The CGs were usually willing to oblige in allowing me sufficient time to be flown the required safe distance from the scene. Then their natural curiosity ensured they examined the cards. Without exception, any picture of a dinosaur — realistic-looking or a cuddly 'Barney' type — would cause unmistakable symptoms of trigger syndrome in a genuine CG.

After the test, the location would be examined. A positive test result will have caused a frozen bloodbath. Dead penguins, walruses, fish and all other deceased life forms would litter the surface of the snow and ice or be floating in the surrounding deep-red sea. Do not be fooled into believing the declining number of polar bears is in any way linked to climate change. I am ashamed to say this is something I must accept responsibility for.

CHAPTER NINE
DANCING WITH DAVID

Nobody does it better, and what an incredible dancer he is! I saw him moonwalking and doing his 'shimmy'. I knew him to be a great broadcaster and richly deserving of his 'British institution' accolade, but Sir David Attenborough, breakdancing at the age of seventy-seven! Sir David told me, following the afterparty, that the CGs had provided him with a renewed zest for life and that he felt 'like a new man'. This high-energy 'bash' took place in 2003, after filming Attenborough's natural history series *Wild Women on One*. With live music performed by Skylie and the Pussycat Trolls, it was a fitting celebration of the yearlong making of Sir David's series documentary, made with my assistance, covering the remarkable story of the Cave Girls from their beginning to the present day. I believed that I had finally convinced the prime minister of the day, Tony Blair, that the time had arrived for the curtain covering these women be lifted.

Tony appeared positive to my suggestion for this to be achieved by way of a documentary narrated by Sir David. The distinctive authority with which he communicates would deliver the profoundly serious message to the man in the street, that one of these remarkable and dangerous beings may live next door. Yet, the perfect pitch to his words makes his listeners concentrate on the smallest detail. This is important as, if a state of emergency were declared in the

UK, instructions regarding personal safety would be readily absorbed by viewers.

With the prime minister's apparent blessing, the BBC was commissioned to create what the government dubbed 'a public information message'. Before filming commenced, I urged Attenborough to, as far as was possible, sound 'reassuring' to the audience as widespread public panic could 'force the hand' of the CGs into taking incredibly positive and undesirable actions. Also, if the television broadcasts were made appealing to any CGs watching at home, they would be more likely to remain passive.

What a coup the BBC had landed! At least, so it appeared to its top hierarchy. Secret senior-level negotiations between the government and the corporation, led to the making of a twenty-episode series in which, at the very height of his career, Sir David would narrate the remarkable story that mankind never has been top of the food chain, and throughout our existence on Earth, a vastly superior species has been laughing at us and our behaviour. With the Beeb granted exclusivity in breaking the bombshell, it would ensure record ratings. Sir David whispered at the meeting, 'I feel so privileged to have been chosen for this, Crawford. This is the absolute pinnacle for me. It just eclipses almost anything else that has ever been shown on television: the first nuclear explosion, man on the moon, the shooting of Kennedy. Finally, I will be able to tell the people of Britain exactly what Anne Robinson is.'

With the women ready, the cameras rolled. Every type of brick-built construction was erected and smashed, huge inflatable reptiles were savagely mutilated, and Nicola swam around the planet in a disappointing time of fifteen seconds. However, she had stopped to pick up some lunch, so that she could treat the film crew to a culinary delight... barbecued orca with lemon and herb, served with new potatoes. Sufficiently divine; Ainsley Harriott would have been envious. Key moments were captured: Bigfoot being treated to a pedicure and Skylie spinning around at such velocity that the resulting friction evaporated the water in Loch Ness, exposing... yes, you know who!

Attenborough was in his element, liberated from humdrum narrations on ants in the forests, dung beetles, or the mating rituals of hyenas. Now he was describing how modern man had carved ancient hill figures such as the Long Man of Wilmington, in East Sussex and the Cerne Giant in Dorset, with the intention of frightening the CGs. However, they laughed at the men's feeble efforts. In revenge, the girls made a giant, animated hologram of a Cave Girl making stabbing motions with a spear. The terrifying, three-dimensional image looked down from the heavens before walking across the sky. Visible from anywhere on Earth for three months, it forced every form of life, even the most minute bacteria particles, into 'lock down', remaining out of sight and inactive, until the girls were satisfied the men had learned their lesson. After explaining how ancient civilisations were destroyed and entire modern military regiments were wiped out by single CGs, Sir David would create his favourite episode of *Wild Women on One*: the episode that included aliens from outer space!

Uncharacteristically, the legendary broadcaster was unable to check his excitement. The emotion was clear in his voice as he narrated how, millions of years ago, planet Earth was regularly visited by small humanoid-looking creatures that had travelled in spacecrafts resembling the stereotypical 'flying saucers' that we have seen in comic books. The aliens, known as 'Pukants', were pale green in colour, bald with two large, black eyes. They were an advanced species who came from the planet Corbynia. Similar in size to Venus, it lay thirty billion light years from Earth. CGs at first tolerated Pukants, until the girls discovered the creatures were leaving circles in the fields of crops, known as crop circles. Often the crops had been flattened and ornate pattens left in the fields. As this was damaging the cereal-making plants, the women became incensed and waited in ambush for the flying saucers to return.

The first one landed and made what was to be its last crop circle. Ascending back towards space at a speed of warp factor four, a CG grabbed hold of the alien craft, halting its progress in an instant and pulled it back down to the ground. The little green men, desperate to escape, activated the defence laser. However, the Cave Girl simply turned the vessel to one side, thus changing the direction of the laser beam to shoot down the three flying saucers that were responding to the distress call the original had sent.

With a group of CGs now in the fields, the girls played with the first alien craft. The design of the flying saucer made it the perfect giant frisbee for the ladies to skim through the air at one another. They really enjoyed the exercise and then increased the intensity, making it a rigorous physical workout. After a while, they prised open the spacecraft like an oyster to investigate the effects on those little green people. Well, they had become liquidised and the girls laughed as the green slime oozed from a gap in the now-damaged craft.

Sir David explained in the series how, during the night, the women discovered that 'Pukant slime' is phosphorescent. The slime was also highly radioactive, yet it was perfect for decorating the roofs of houses and trees at Christmas time. After the festive season, the slime remained in place as it proved more effective than solar panels. The women later discovered the substance was a suitable fuel for supercharged motor vehicles. The concept of 'green energy' was first spawned, all those years ago, by Cave Girls! Transforming Pukants into slime caught on in a big way. When the aliens began avoiding Earth, the CGs decided to hunt them on Corbynia instead. Shaken vigorously, Pukants produced copious amounts of slime. Visitors from outer space were once an everyday occurrence, but the women succeeded in stopping almost all visits of this nature. The last one was to Roswell, New Mexico, in 1947. Even then, the women reached the alien sooner than the US Air Force, who disposed of the corpse.

The series was made. The public would finally learn the dark secret of the Cave Girls. Yet, six months before *Wild Women on One* was to be aired, Tony Blair held a meeting with Greg Dyke, the then director-general of the BBC. Dyke was told that, 'due to a change of heart', the series must be pulled. Credit where it is due, Dyke was unrestrained in displaying his displeasure at government interference and the questions it would raise regarding BBC political impartiality. With the relationship between the government and the corporation at an all-time low, Sir

David was informed that his unique ground-breaking production had been axed. The poor fellow was so devastated I became genuinely concerned for him. Nicola suggested I invite him round to Whitehall. Graciously accepting my invitation, Attenborough enjoyed a relaxing alcoholic beverage with the ladies, but I still felt sorry for David. He was to be relegated to BBC2 for a new series, *Wildlife on Two*, where he could safely tell us all more about the butterflies of Belarus and the woodlice of Watford. However, a glint returned to his eyes when Nicola said, 'David, we had so much fun together.' In a moment almost reminiscent of a scene from the film *Dirty Dancing*, David Swayze Attenborough took hold of Nicola's hand, who in return, lifted Sir David from the floor. With his body now horizontal above her head, he looked into Nicola's eyes and said softly, 'I had the time of my life.'

CHAPTER TEN
HAPPILY, EVER AFTER?

'You lazy good-for-nothing, get your butt back to work by ten am. today. I don't care that your back is broken, or that your spinal cord was severed in a workplace accident yesterday. You are not dead, so go to work!' Ruby was ranting as I entered the Welfare Office in the Human Resources Department of Thames Wide Building Society. The handset of the telephone shattered into plastic splinters as she angrily slammed it down on the dialler. 'Now look what he made me do. People who don't want to work make me so cross. I've only been the head of welfare an hour and this is the third telephone I've broken!'

'I've finally caught up with you, Ruby. My sources suggested I would find you teaching the five-year-olds at the Mixed Martial Arts Centre down the road but the manager told me you had left. Apparently, you were teaching them so well they were beating up their schoolteachers. The head of science is in a coma. Now, it is time for you to come back with me to HQ. You have had long enough on your own.'

To be honest, I had not realised CG Ruby was missing until the matter was discovered during the annual audit. The knives had long been out for me, but a mislaid 'annihilation machine' was just the excuse required in demanding my resignation. For years, I had been uneasy at being complicit with government over the use and secrecy of the Cave Girls.

History books filled with half-truths, even universities denying the existence of these women. I was tired of the lies, and the government knew this. Every dog has its day; mine had been and gone, along with my prospects of that knighthood.

I would like to say that I enjoyed every minute working with the girls, but that would not be accurate. However, I did have much fun and few regrets really. In the line of duty, I have travelled extensively around the world. Halfway through a six-hour flight with gaffe-prone Donald Trump, the president commented, whilst eating a cheese and pickle sandwich, 'We never really cracked fast food delivery in America. If we had, I would be eating a McDonald's now.' Less than five minutes later, a Happy Meal was placed in front of him by a woman. The CG had overheard Trump whilst she was in a McDonald's restaurant. She teleported herself onto Air Force One. The look I witnessed on his face was priceless, and he loved the toy action figure included. Half an hour after landing, a presidential aide tentatively reminded the president that the aircraft had landed, to which he received the full lash of Trump's tongue when he shouted, 'Well, I'm still playing with my Power Ranger!' Donald was even more ridiculous than most realise. I will always remember during one of our appointments, he was bellowing at a team of government scientists, 'Do it! Just do it. Inject her into my veins!' A huge needle syringe containing a giggling CG had been suspended from a metal beam that was being lowered towards Trump with a rope and pulley. Believing that injecting the female into his body would provide permanent immunity against all present and future disease, the president was becoming increasingly irritated with his personal doctor's lack of enthusiasm. Reluctantly, Donald succumbed to the medical advice and the girl was injected into what is now a dangerously aggressive and indestructible laboratory rat. That said, the creature does provide telephone support to mobile refrigeration engineers working throughout the United States.

My close encounters with many heads of state, royalty, prime ministers, police chiefs, celebrities and, not least, the women themselves, have enriched my life beyond imagination. They have increased my knowledge tenfold. I have unlearned what I previously considered to be the facts regarding evolution and history and hope that I have now been able to educate you, despite the brainwashing barrage that you have been exposed to since birth. Much of my work has been invaluable, and to the fans of Millwall Football Club, you should be especially grateful. Misunderstandings occur every day. What happened at the T Rex concert began with a misunderstanding. Let me tell you, having the nickname 'The Lions', who even play at a stadium called 'The Den', was for many years, just red rag to a bull! With the reputation of, let's say, some of your fans (deservedly or not), I believed a 'trigger situation' was looming. A situation that would make the very hardest of hooligans quake in their bovver boots. Therefore, I worked tirelessly to persuade all known CGs that Millwall is a football club whose team is supported by very nice and gentle people. So next time you are at a match chanting "No one likes us, we don't care", please remember that Professor Bond did his very best for you!

Although Cave Girls are physically fit and armed with

remarkable athletic and mental abilities, they may come in all shapes and sizes. The CG gene does not discriminate either, regarding ethnicity or skin colouring. There is no typical Cave Girl; they strive to be inclusive and embrace diversity amongst themselves. International governments are fully aware that some of these girls are living amongst the masses. For this reason, you, my friend, have a part to play. Humanity is in a more precarious state than you may realise. You must avoid all arguments where possible, including 'road rage' situations. If your eyes meet those of a lady walking towards you and she asks, 'What are you looking at?' then run! Most importantly, refrain from making crop circles, no matter how tempting this may be. This is foolhardy and highly dangerous.

On a personal note, I am in the rudest of health, as is my friend Henry. Skylie and friends agreed to provide him with some medical procedures they pioneered when dinosaurs walked the Earth, to make Henry as good as new. Their actions here illustrate that the women can appear to show a degree of compassion. However, I am more than a little concerned at the news that wild bison will be reintroduced to England in spring 2022. Six thousand years ago, the girls did not think they should be in the country and may not be pleased that someone else thinks better. Many years ago, when the matter was first proposed, Nicola's exact words were, 'You lot really are playing with fire.'

I should now be retired, enjoying my garden, instead of hiding from the sinister, dark figures who lurk in the shadows, waiting for the moment to assassinate me 'in the best interests of queen and country'. However, I try not to be bitter. I am far more tolerant and accepting of others now.

The fact that I only wince and chastise folk with the Brummie dialect is testament to this. Regrettably, I never visited the planet Corbynia. I will just tell you that Corbynia regularly stages The Annual CG Music Awards. I've heard some particularly favourable comments on a new group called the Hooababes. Katy had promised to 'whisk me away there' with her. Apparently, the atmosphere and climate are highly beneficial to the skin. My only recreation these days is dusting off the old Trippier 908, connecting my new surround sound system and dancing along to the music and 'video' of Skylie and the Pussycat Trolls, while thinking of poor old Sir David Attenborough as he now tries to convince even himself that our greatest challenges centre around climate change!

Printed in Great Britain
by Amazon

79552522R00062